BBC DOCTOR WHO

Plague City

BBC

DOCTOR WHO

Plague City

Jonathan Morris

BOOKS

3 5 7 9 10 8 6 4

BBC Books, an imprint of Ebury Publishing
20 Vauxhall Bridge Road,
London SW1V 2SA

BBC Books is part of the Penguin Random House group of companies
whose addresses can be found at global.penguinrandomhouse.com

Penguin
Random House
UK

Doctor Who is a BBC Wales production for BBC One.
Executive producers: Steven Moffat and Brian Minchin

First published by BBC Books in 2017

www.eburypublishing.co.uk

Editorial Director: Albert DePetrillo
Copyeditor: Steve Tribe
Series consultant: Justin Richards
Cover design: Lee Binding © Woodlands Books Ltd, 2017
Production: Alex Merrett

A CIP catalogue record for this book is available from the British Library

ISBN 9781785942709

Printed and bound in Great Britain by Clays Ltd, St Ives PLC

Penguin Random House is committed to a sustainable future for
our business, our readers and our planet. This book is made
from Forest Stewardship Council® certified paper.

To Alexander

Chapter

I

It was the sound they had been dreading. Four slow, heavy thuds on their tenement door. The sound meant only one thing: their daughter, Catherine, would not live to see another dawn. She was only 19, little more than a girl. She didn't deserve to die.

Thomas had feared the worst ever since Catherine had shown the first symptoms four days ago. She had complained of feeling faint and tired, which was most unlike her, and she had retired early to bed. The next morning she was even weaker, gasping and shivering with the cold even after they moved her bed to beside the hearth, stoked up the fire and covered her with every blanket they owned. But over the next two days she fell into a terrible fever. She suffered coughing fits that caused her to double up in pain and panted for air as though she had run the length of Canongate Street. Her nightclothes clung to her, damp with sweat, and she drifted in and out of a tortured sleep and a fretful delirium, calling for water and calling for her ma and pa to stay close and hold her hand.

Thomas was holding her hand now, gently rubbing her limp fingers to keep them warm. She was asleep finally, which was a blessing, but her breathing remained laboured, her lungs cracking like a pair of bellows. Even by the flickering half-light of the fire, he could make out her sore, reddened eyelids and the paleness of her cheeks. She was always a very pale girl, just like her mother, but now her skin was so transparent he could make out the veins in her temples. And, on her lily-smooth neck below her ears, the festering red blisters that marked her out as a victim of the plague.

She had grown weaker with each hour that passed and now the knock at the door confirmed her fate. Soon she would be dead and he would never hear the sound of her voice again; never hear her laughter, never see her smile. He would never see her dance again, laughing with delight as she hoisted her petticoat, her chin raised, flicking her long, dark, wavy hair behind her. He would never see her marry; she would never have children; she would never grow old. Just the thought of losing her was like having a great beast gnawing at his stomach, a weight pressing down upon his heart. The dread of all the bleak and empty days to come made him feel like he was choking.

There were four more knocks at the door. Thomas released his daughter's hand and stood up. Seated on the other side of the hearth, Isobel looked at him imploringly. 'Dinnae.'

'What choice have we got?' said Thomas. He steeled himself to open the door. 'You ken what they say. He's no' going to gie up, he's no' gonnae go away.'

Isobel turned away and resumed stirring the pottage in the cauldron over the fire. Thomas unbolted and slowly opened the door. A gust of icy air blew into the room, making the fire snap and growl like a dog facing an unwelcome guest. Thomas shuddered, but not from the cold. Outside on the landing of the eighth floor stood a figure from his nightmares. The Night Doctor.

The figure lowered the metal staff it had used to knock on the door and turned its masked, long-beaked face towards him. It regarded him blankly, the wearer's eyes hidden behind the mask's eyeholes. For reasons known only to the wearer, the mask had been sculpted in the form of a giant raven's skull and was topped with a flat, wide-brimmed hat. Beneath it a loose-fitting leather robe hung down like the wings of a bat, concealing the wearer's legs and feet, while a chinstrap extended from the hat to secure the hood of the robe to the mask and ensure that no part of the wearer's head was left exposed. Its hands were protected with falconry gauntlets with long nails attached to each finger.

The figure indicated with a flourish of a talon-like hand that it wished to enter. Thomas backed into his tenement, and the figure lowered its head to pass through the door. It stood over a foot taller than Thomas and when it pulled itself upright there was barely an inch gap between its hat and the rafters. It looked left and right as though searching before it registered the presence of the girl sleeping by the fire.

'No,' said Isobel, her voice breaking into a sob. 'Please.'

Thomas closed the door and pulled up a chair beside his wife, placing an arm around her for comfort. She was quaking with fear and he softly shushed her as the Night Doctor approached Catherine's bed. It moved in absolute silence, without the sound of a single footstep or the creak of a single floorboard. It was as if it had sucked all the noise from the room, save for the crackle of the fire and Catherine's feeble, hoarse breathing.

As the figure passed him, Thomas could smell a pungent mixture of honeysuckle, heather and other herbs. Combined with the oily aroma of the Night Doctor's damp cloak, the effect was overpowering, and Thomas covered his mouth to stop himself gagging.

The Night Doctor didn't examine Catherine. Instead, it used its staff to pull back the blankets, then slowly let the point of the staff drift along her body until it was directly over her forehead. The Night Doctor let it hover there for what seemed like an hour, then abruptly drew it back and turned to go.

'Is there no hope for her?' asked Isobel.

The Night Doctor stared at Isobel for a moment as though it did not understand the question. Thomas gazed into its glass eyes for some clue of what lay beneath the mask, but all he could see was the reflection of the fire. Then the Night Doctor strode to the door, opened it, and ducked outside, letting the wind slam the door in its wake.

Isobel tidied Catherine's blankets and tenderly stroked her daughter's hair. 'She's no' deid,' she said quietly. 'She might still recover.'

Thomas closed the door. 'They say anyone visited by the Night Doctor—'

'I ken what they say, Thomas Abney. But that disnae mean they're right. That disnae mean he's right about our Cathy.'

'Isobel—'

'I ken my own daughter and she's a bonnie wee lass, with sae much life in her. She'll pull through, I ken she will. She'll prove thon doctor wrong. We just hae to trust to the mercy o' the Lord'.

Thomas kissed his wife on the forehead. Like him, she had hardly slept for the last four days, and her eyes were sore from exhaustion and weeping. Her hair, which had begun to turn to grey the year before, was now pure grey and as fine as raw flax, as though she had aged ten years over the past week.

Catherine's condition did not improve. Over the next two hours, her breathing grew ever more strained and

5

desperate, like someone rescued from drowning, using all her energy to suck air into her lungs. Thomas and Isobel did their best to make her comfortable, plumping up the straw under her head, wiping her brow, dampening her lips with wet linen. They prayed for her to be spared by the Lord's grace, for her to be forgiven for the sins that had brought this punishment upon her. But it made no difference. Thomas had seen people die before; his parents, his brothers, his friends. He had seen the plague do its work, he knew its pattern of death, and he knew that if Catherine had been chosen to be one of the few to survive she would have shown signs of recovery by now. Instead, her fever remained high, the blisters on her neck swelled as large as crab-apples and her fingertips turned as black as coal.

Then Thomas heard the footsteps coming up the stairwell, followed by the knock at the door. Four slow, heavy thuds. The Night Doctor had returned. Thomas looked at his wife. She grimaced with the pain of holding back the tears, mouthing 'No'.

There were four more knocks at the door. Thomas opened it, to see the Night Doctor standing in the light before dawn. The Night Doctor waved a gloved hand, indicating that it desired to enter. Thomas stepped out of its way, and the Night Doctor walked in and surveyed the room with its blank, glass eyes.

'What is it? You've already seen her, what dae you want?' Thomas asked.

By way of an answer, the Night Doctor crossed the room and leaned over Catherine's sleeping form, so close that its long, copper beak nearly touched her face.

'No,' said Isobel. 'You can't. You cannae take her.'

The Night Doctor drew back the blankets with its claw-like hands and lifted Catherine from the bed. She let out a short, croaking gasp as her head lolled back, her body hanging limply in the Night Doctor's arms.

'Leave her be,' whimpered Isobel. 'Please. Just let her die here.'

The Night Doctor gazed at Isobel with its blank, glass eyes, and slowly shook its head from side to side. Then it carried Catherine to the door, which Thomas, in his reverie, was still holding open. Catherine let out another gasp as the cloaked figure stooped to pass through the door without dislodging its hat. Then it descended the stairs, its boots clacking on each of the stone steps. Thomas watched the figure carrying his daughter away until it reached the corner of the stairwell and disappeared from view.

Then Thomas returned to his sobbing wife, and his daughter's empty bed.

'She's away,' said Isobel plaintively, before the grief overcame her. 'She's away.'

Thomas placed his hand on her shoulder. He had to be strong for her, to stand tall, like an oak in a storm. But all he could feel was the great beast gnawing at his stomach.

Chapter

2

Chapter

2

Her heart pounding with excitement, Bill shoved open the TARDIS doors and ran out into a dark, narrow alleyway. It smelt of damp, like a castle dungeon, mixed with the stench of rotting vegetables that Bill knew only too well from the occasions she had had to empty the canteen's bins. And there was something else: the unmistakable stench of manure. One of the gutters that ran alongside the cobblestones was practically an open cesspit.

'Doctor?' called Bill into the TARDIS. 'Are you sure this is Edinburgh? I mean, I've never been, but, you know, it's a little bit grimmer than it looks on telly.'

'Don't worry, the TARDIS may be marginally off course,' replied the Doctor from inside the TARDIS. 'It's probably just Leith.'

'I think we might be more than marginally,' said Bill, looking up. The alleyway was barely wider than the TARDIS, and grew narrower as it extended upwards and the stone walls gave way to wooden beams and crumbling plaster. No, not plaster, thought Bill, remembering her history. Wattle and daub. Each storey overhung the one beneath, so by the fifth level the gap thirty centimetres wide each building and the one opposite was only a foot wide, leaving no view of the sky. Grey sheets hung from several of the windows, while others were shuttered or boarded up.

Bill grinned. Going by the buildings, they had travelled back hundreds of years. This was probably the Middle Ages. Shakespeare times!

'We're in history!'

'We're always in history. Even in the future, it's still history. It depends how you look at it.' The Doctor emerged from the TARDIS and frowned. 'It's not supposed to look like this?'

'No.'

'Oh. It's your planet, you're the expert,' shrugged the Doctor. 'But all cities have their dark alleys, their backstreets. Just because it's an assault on the olfactory organs doesn't mean it's necessarily the past.'

'If this is Edinburgh, I'm guessing the Royal Mile is that way,' said Bill, pointing to where the alleyway sloped upwards. 'Come on!'

A cough came from behind them. Bill turned to see Nardole in the TARDIS doorway wearing his ever-present duffel coat along with a Minnie the Minx beret –

what was it they were called? A tam-o'-shanter – and a kilt complete with sporran. Nardole beamed, inviting comment.

'No, don't do that,' said the Doctor.

'Don't do what?' said Nardole, perplexed.

'That.' The Doctor waved in the direction of the hat and kilt. 'They'll think you're being sarcastic. You'll be lucky to get away with a punch in the face.'

Nardole cleared his throat diplomatically. 'You wish me to deny my heritage?'

'Your what?

'My heritage,' Nardole repeated. 'You forget. I am descended from the clan MacNardole.' Bill giggled, which Nardole acknowledged with a gracious nod, before gesturing downwards with the utmost seriousness. 'You see. I even wear the MacNardole tartan.'

'MacNardole?' The Doctor sighed. 'We're *all* going to get punched in the face.' He raised his head to shout up at the windows. 'We're not with him! He's no' with us!'

'I don't see why I can't be Scottish,' muttered Nardole.

'Because you're an alien. You're not from this planet, least of all Scotland. You … you don't even have the right accent!'

'And you do?'

'That's entirely different.'

'I don't see why you get to be Scottish and I don't,' said Nardole. 'Perhaps I should do the accent too? Ah dinnae ken, ah sleekit cowerin' timorous wee haggis awn ma pleet …'

'No,' said the Doctor. 'Do that, you'll probably start a small war.' He addressed the surrounding windows. 'Honestly, he's a total stranger, we've literally just met! We don't like him very much either!'

'Fine, fine,' said Nardole. 'I *anticipated* this eventuality.' He removed his tam-o'-shanter, stuck it in his coat pocket, and took his normal woolly hat from another pocket and stuck it on his head. Then he dug into another pocket and retrieved his trousers with a flourish like a stage magician. He reached down to undo his kilt, then paused. 'Don't mind me. You go ahead,' he said, waving the Doctor and Bill away. 'I'll catch you up. Shoo, shoo!'

Bill gave Nardole a sympathetic smile and dashed up the alleyway, taking care to avoid ruining her trainers in the drainage ditch. The alleyway ended in a set of steps, which opened into a street wide enough for Bill to see the sky. It was overcast, streaked with the red of a sunset. Or a sunrise, Bill corrected herself. The cold air and dampness indicated it was … well, if they *were* in Edinburgh, it could be any time of the year, really.

Bill looked back to check the Doctor was still with her, then piled out onto a wide street. And halted. The street was lined with blocks upward of a dozen storeys high, bulging over the road and squeezed together like hardbacks on a bookshelf. Whoever lived in these places was doing all right, as they all had glass windows and ground-floor stables. On the other hand, maybe they weren't doing all right any more, because the paint was cracked and half the doors were boarded up with rough timber.

The street was utterly deserted. There weren't even any birds. The grey buildings stood like mourners at a graveside. It had been abandoned for so long that weeds and wild flowers were pushing up between the flagstones.

Bill spoke softly, as though talking too loudly would be disrespectful. 'There's nobody here. I was expecting jugglers and blokes on stilts.'

'It *is* Edinburgh, though,' said the Doctor, pointing at a building like a cross between a town hall and a medieval castle which blocked off half the street. 'That's the Heart of Midlothian. And there –' he indicated towards a huge, brooding gothic church – 'St Giles' Cathedral.'

'Wrong century, then,' said Bill.

'Do you have any idea how difficult it is, in the vastness of creation, to get the right planet, never mind the right city? You have to allow a little … leeway. A few hundred years is barely the blink of an eye as far as the universe is concerned. Plus, look on the bright side.'

'Which is?'

'No jugglers or blokes on stilts.'

'You can say that again. This place is completely—'

'Bring out yer deid!' called out a gruff, male voice, accompanied by the clanging of a bell. 'Bring out

13

yer deid! We'll be wanting yer deid!' A group of men emerged from a side street, all dressed in tunics with red crosses on the front and back. Their leader, a mournful-looking man with the heavy jowls of a bulldog, waved a cloth on the end of a staff. He was followed by the bell-ringer, while the rest of his men pushed a large cart laden with what at first looked like sacks of potatoes. But then Bill noticed the legs and arms hanging limply amongst the sacks, the skin marked with black blotches.

She exchanged a wary glance with the Doctor, and noticed that they'd been joined by an anxious Nardole, now in trousers.

'They don't look well,' Nardole observed.

'Plague,' said the Doctor grimly. 'I take it back. Jugglers are better.'

'Bring out yer deid!' shouted the bell-ringer. One of the doors on the street swung open to reveal a thin, terrified woman with wild hair and eyes. Before she said a word, the bulldog-faced man yelled at her to go back inside. She disappeared from view, then two of the men in robes pulled rags over their noses and mouths and went into the building. Moments later, they emerged carrying the corpse of a white-haired old man, which they dumped onto the cart.

The woman reappeared in the doorway. Even from a distance, Bill could hear her pleas and the bulldog-faced man telling her that she could not leave her home. He shoved her inside and pulled the door shut, then waved forward a hungry-looking teenage boy who handed him a hammer. The man hammered a nail into the door and hung upon it a cloth with a blood-red cross.

Bill was about to suggest to the Doctor that they leave when the bulldog-faced man registered their presence. 'What in the name dae you think you're doing?'

'We were just wondering,' the Doctor called back. 'What day is bins?'

The bulldog man nodded to two of his men. They didn't look like soldiers; they had coarse, lined faces like fishermen or shepherds, men who spent their whole lives braving the elements. But nevertheless they each unsheathed a thin sword as they advanced towards them. 'Dae you no' ken there's a curfew?' said the bulldog-faced man.

'A what?' said Bill.

'Naebody is allowed out after sunset. On pain o' death.'

'You're out.'

'We're Baileys o' the Muir. We're allowed.'

'It's not sunset yet. Technically. Still daylight. Just saying.'

'I'm sorry,' interjected the Doctor. 'We weren't aware of your little rule.'

'But we are now,' said Nardole, tapping the side of his head. 'All up here.'

'We realise curfews are terribly important things which must be enforced rigorously,' continued the Doctor. 'So if it's all right with you fine gentlemen, we'll get out of your hair and find somewhere indoors to be.' The Doctor grasped Bill's hand and turned to head back down the alleyway.

'Haud on,' said the bulldog man. 'How can you no' ken 'bout the curfew?'

'We … haven't got out much?' said the Doctor. '… Because of the curfew?'

'We've chapped on every door in this town, every day the past month,' said the bulldog man. 'All the gates are guarded. The only way you wouldnae ken … would be if you'd come in o'er the wall.'

One of the soldiers pointed at Bill with his sword and gave a cough. 'Looks Barbary to me. Must hae come off a ship in Leith.'

'What did you call me?' said Bill, her temper rising.

'I think,' the Doctor whispered to her, his grip on her hand tightening, 'this might be a conversation best continued in the TARDIS.'

'He means *run!*' said Nardole helpfully. Arms waving, he jogged back to the alleyway – just as the door of one of the houses swung open. Nardole halted in his tracks as a man staggered out, stripped to the waist, his chest and stomach covered in livid sores. His eyes were bloodshot, and his hair and beard looked as though he had been tearing at them.

'We are forsaken!' the man snarled. 'The Day of Judgement approaches!'

'If you say so!' said Nardole, putting up his hands to humour the delirious man. He might not be infectious, but he looked like he could turn violent. And he was between them and the way back to the TARDIS.

'Split up,' said the Doctor.

'What?' said Bill.

'I'll find you. Run!'

The Doctor released Bill's hand and she ran down the street, her feet tripping over the cobbles. She glanced back to see the Doctor and Nardole disappearing down one of the side streets with two soldiers in pursuit. Two more of the soldiers were after her, while their leader fended off the delirious man.

Bill didn't look back again. She sprinted towards an alleyway on the left, which she guessed would run parallel to the one with the TARDIS. The alleyway sloped steeply downwards, the flagstones giving way to muddy steps. As the overhanging storeys of the houses cut out the remaining daylight, Bill found herself running through almost total darkness – and once again sidestepping a treacherous drainage channel. The alleyway became a tunnel narrow enough for Bill to keep her balance by trailing her hands along both walls. The tunnel twisted sharply to the right, and for a moment Bill feared it would be a dead end. Instead, it split into two. Bill turned left, down a steep set of steps into an even narrower street. Her trainers splashed in what she desperately hoped was just a muddy puddle. The street turned to the right again, before ending in a courtyard, no more than ten metres across, surrounded by high tenements. She could hear the soldiers shouting 'She went this way', 'Doon here!' They were getting closer. And she was trapped.

She looked around for an escape route. The walls were rough enough to grip, but even if she could climb up, the overhanging second storey would make it impossible to get any higher. She glanced into a nearby barrel which was full of rotting fish and chicken bones, more of a compost heap than a potential hiding place.

'We've got her!' one of the soldiers laughed.

Any second now, they would be turning the corner. She had a choice. Either she could fight … or surrender.

'In here, pet,' said a grandmotherly voice behind her.

Bill turned to see an old woman with a long, thin nose standing in a doorway, waving for her to join her inside. Bill didn't think twice. She smiled at the woman and ran into the building. The woman closed the door behind her and put it on the latch, then lifted a finger to her lips to indicate for Bill to remain quiet.

Bill could hear the soldiers in the alleyway outside. 'She's gone the other way!' one of them barked. 'You lost her, you eejit! Come on!' They hurried away, their boots clomping into the distance.

Bill felt the woman's fingernails on her shoulder, and allowed herself to be guided up a winding staircase to a room on the fifth storey. A crackling fire in the hearth filled it with heat, the smell of smoke and a flickering glow. Another old woman sat beside it in a rocking chair. She had a hard, weathered face. Bill guessed her to be about eighty, but then thought again. People in the past aged quicker, she was probably only fifty.

'Hello?' said the woman by the fire.

'We hae a guest, Agnes,' explained the woman behind Bill. She collected a poker and jabbed it into the fire. 'She was fleeing frae the Bailey, would ye credit it!'

'Yeah, thanks for that,' said Bill, wiping whatever was on her shoes on the doormat.

'What did they want wi' ye?' asked Agnes, her eyes narrowing.

'My bad, I didn't realise there was a "curfew". I'm new around here.'

'Aye, they'd only hae to take a look at you to ken that,' said the other woman. 'But why would anyone want to come here? The town is in … whit's the word? French.'

'Quarantine,' said Agnes.

'Aye. That's it. Quarantine.'

'It was a mistake.' Bill took in the room, which had black drapes over the walls and no furniture save for two rocking chairs and a wooden table. 'We didn't know about the plague.'

'You didnae ken? So you've no' been touched by it?' said Agnes.

'Touched by it? No. I ... I don't even know if I can catch it. BCG.'

'Maybe we should gie her a looking-over, Betsy?'

'A looking-over?' said Bill. The two women were staring at her like she'd been caught shoplifting, the flickering firelight reflecting in their accusing eyes. Why were they looking at her like that? All hungry, like. 'No, I'm fine. Really, I am. But if you want me gone—'

'That'll no' be needed,' said Betsy, offering her one of the chairs. 'Warm yersel. See, concealing anyone with the sickness is punishable by death.' As she spoke, she gave Agnes a glance full of meaning.

'Like a lot of things around here.' Bill sat down, trying not to meet Agnes's accusing gaze. 'You'd think they'd want to save life, what with the plague.'

'That's why they're sae hard,' said Betsy. 'Out o' fear.'

'They're scared?'

'It's bad here, but in other parts they say there's mair with the plague than no'.'

'Hence the quarantine?'

'Awbody is to stay in their houses, to stop the spread,' said Agnes, with a slight smile as though she relished the idea. 'Thon men, if they'd caught you, they'd hae you branded or banished. That's if you were lucky. So you're stuck with us both for the night.'

Bill felt Betsy's hand on her shoulder. She didn't find it entirely reassuring.

Chapter

3

A boom of thunder reverberated across the rooftops. Nardole looked up at the cloud-covered sky, into the rain sluicing down like a waterfall. He shivered and turned to the Doctor, sheltering in the archway beside him. 'Nice weather for Anatids,' he said, trying to lighten the mood.

'I thought I told you to split up,' said the Doctor. 'Why are you still with me?'

'Yes,' said Nardole. 'I thought I'd split up … with you.'

After leaving the High Street, they had made their way through a series of backstreets and dark, winding stairways until they had lost not only their pursuers but, as far as Nardole could tell, themselves. Then it had started to rain, and as the last glows of sunset disappeared from the sky, the city sank into an impenetrable darkness.

'Hope Bill's all right.'

'She'll be fine. She should have found her way back at the TARDIS by now.'

'And if she hasn't?'

'Then she could be anywhere.'

'Not much chance of finding her in this,' Nardole sighed. 'It's not as if we can go around knocking on doors.'

'No …' The Doctor trailed off.

Nardole followed his gaze, to see a young woman striding towards them through the rain dressed in a plain white robe. She had pale skin and her hair clung to her back, damp and black like tangled seaweed. She looked at them with imploring, haunted eyes.

'Can ye help me?' said the woman. 'I'm feart. I want my ma and da.'

'Of course,' said the Doctor. 'Anything we can do. Where are they?'

The woman slowly raised her right arm upwards. 'In there.'

Nardole looked up, squinting into the downpour, and estimated she was pointing to one of the upper floors of the tenement, seven or eight storeys up. He realised they were standing in the building entrance and stepped aside while the Doctor tried the door. It was locked, so he pulled out his sonic screwdriver and buzzed it until the iron lock clicked and clanked. The door swung open, revealing an incredibly steep, winding stairwell.

Without a word of thanks, the woman strode through the doorway. Nardole backed out of her way, affronted, and she walked inside and began to climb the stairs, quickly disappearing from view.

Nardole exchanged a bewildered glance with the Doctor. 'Rude,' said Nardole. 'She's lucky we were here. Out in this, she'd be lucky not to catch her death.'

'Quite.' The Doctor darted inside and scampered up the stairs. With a sigh, Nardole hurried after him.

They came to a landing with three boarded-up doors. There was no sign of the girl, not even any footprints, so they kept going up the stairs, coming to another empty landing. The Doctor quickened the pace, darting up the next flight of stairs and the next until they emerged onto the landing of the eighth floor, which consisted of a short passage leading to a single wooden door, barely visible in the gloom.

'She must've gone into one of the flats,' said Nardole.

'I suppose so,' said the Doctor. 'We can hardly have missed her.'

'Why the sudden interest? I mean, I'm not one to judge, you have form, but …'

'Didn't you notice?'

'Notice what?'

The Doctor was about to reply when a man's voice barked out of the doorway. 'Awa yerselves!'

Taken aback, Nardole mouthed 'Oops'. The Doctor raised a hand for silence.

'Awa yerselves,' the man repeated. 'We ken you're out there. Leave us be!'

'Sorry!' the Doctor called back. 'I didn't mean to disturb you.'

There was a pause, then the man replied. 'What are ye? What d'ye want?'

'I'm the Doctor,' said the Doctor. 'Would you mind opening the door, please? So we can continue this conversation without waking up the neighbourhood?'

The door swung open. Inside was a man of about 40, with red hair and a week's beard. He had a heavily lined forehead and sagging eyelids. 'The Doctor?' he said. 'Yer no' the Doctor. Where's thon mask?'

'My mask?' said the Doctor. 'It's hard not to take that personally.'

'Yer bird mask. Aw doctors have bird masks.'

'Ah, well, I'm a little unorthodox in my methods.'

'He is,' said Nardole, backing him up. 'Unorthodox is his middle name. Odd parents.'

'And who's …?' The man indicated Nardole.

'Medical student. Learning on the job.'

This must have satisfied the man, as he ushered them inside. 'In, then, if you're coming. Be quick.'

The Doctor followed the man inside, ducking under the doorway. Nardole followed, helpfully closing the door behind him. He found himself in a small, low-ceilinged room furnished with two chairs, a table and a loom. The kitchen area consisted of a milk churn, a basket of vegetables and an iron hob, with a few bowls and plates stacked on the shelf. A door in the far side led to the sleeping quarters and, going by the smell, whatever served as a bathroom. A small fire in one wall provided a little light and a little heat.

'What is it, Thomas?' said a woman as she entered the room, drawing back her grey hair as she looked quizzically at the Doctor and Nardole.

'This man says he's a doctor,' said Thomas, bolting the door.

'What's he wanting?' said the woman. 'He's too late to dae any guid.'

'Too late?' said the Doctor.

'Our daughter.' Thomas placed a protective arm around the woman Nardole assumed was his wife. 'She died a week afore.'

'The plague?'

Thomas nodded.

'I'm sorry,' said the Doctor.

'There's nae need to apologise,' said Thomas.

'I'm sorry – because I'm going to ask you a few more questions that may be difficult for you to answer. How exactly did she die?'

Looking at the woman, Nardole instinctively felt sorry for her. She had hollow cheeks and red-lined eyes and clearly hadn't slept for weeks. 'She had a fever and she grew waine, till she could scarce draw breath,' she said, matter-of-factly. 'And then the Night Doctor came.'

'The Night Doctor?'

'He took her away.'

'Isobel ...' said Thomas.

Isobel shushed him and continued. 'It's just as they say.'

'What do they say?' said Nardole warily. He had a feeling that he wasn't going to like the answer.

'That anyone visited by the Night Doctor will soon die.'

'Well,' said the Doctor, 'given the survival rate, and the general lack of medical know-how, that doesn't seem that odd.'

'You dinnae understand,' said Isobel. 'Anyone visited by the Night Doctor will perish *that same night*.'

'I see,' said the Doctor. 'With a track record like that, I'm surprised he hasn't been struck off.'

'What?' said Isobel.

'Ignore him,' said Nardole. 'He's not very good with illness, patients ...'

The Doctor prowled around the room, then fixed his eyes back on Thomas and Isobel. 'And she was dead when this "Night Doctor" took her away?'

'No,' said Thomas. 'But she wasnae long for this world.'

'He told you that?'

'No. He never said a word. No' the first time he came, nor two hours later when he came to carry her away.'

'Then – and this may be another upsetting question, so apologies in advance.' The Doctor glanced at Nardole, who nodded to encourage him to keep going. 'But are you sure that she's actually dead?'

'What?' said Isobel.

'If you never saw her die,' said the Doctor.

Thomas and Isobel didn't reply. They just stared at the Doctor indignantly.

The Doctor blew his cheeks in frustration and tried another tack. 'When we were outside, you told us to go away. Did you think I was the Night Doctor?'

'No,' said Thomas.

'No?'

'No. Neither my wife nor I hae the sickness, why would he call on us?'

'Quite,' said the Doctor. He widened his eyes. 'So *who were you expecting?*'

Thomas stood up. 'I dinnae ken what you're proposing, but—'

'No, Thomas,' said Isobel. 'He should ken.' She composed herself, clearing her throat, but before she could speak a voice called from outside.

'Let us in.'

It was the voice of a young woman. Nardole turned to the Doctor, who nodded to indicate he was thinking what Nardole was thinking. They'd heard that voice before.

'Let us in,' the girl repeated.

Thomas took Isobel's hand, as though to defend her.

'It's our Catherine,' said Isobel. 'She's come back.'

'You're sure it's her?' asked the Doctor.

Thomas nodded. 'The first time I opened the door to her, I saw her. But no' again after that, no' ever.'

'Why don't you let her in?' said Nardole. 'If she's got better—'

'She's no' got better,' said Thomas. 'She's ... *unshriven*.'

Nardole was about to ask what that meant when the girl called from outside. 'Please. I'm feart. It's dark out here. Sae dark. I want my ma and da!'

'I cannae bear it,' Isobel cried, burying her head in her husband's chest.

The Doctor took a candle from the mantelpiece. 'Do you mind?' he said, and without waiting for a reply, he lit it from the fire and placed it in a holder. Then he slowly walked towards the door.

'You cannae,' said Thomas.

The girl's voice became a heartrending wail. 'Please, ma and da. Dinnae leave me out here. In the dark.'

The Doctor reached for the latch. 'Don't worry,' he whispered to Thomas. 'I'm not going to let her in.' Then he gestured for Nardole to join him. Nardole shuffled to stand behind him, then the Doctor lifted the latch and pulled the door open.

It took several seconds for Nardole to make out the shape in the darkness. The girl was standing on the far side of the landing, and he could only make her out by the white of her gown. She was facing away from them, looking out through the window into the night, not moving, not breathing as far as Nardole could tell.

Nardole followed the Doctor outside and pulled the door shut behind them. The Doctor raised the candle to head height. The light glistened in the girl's eyes and lent her skin a misty pallor, while casting a shifting shadow on the wall behind her. Her skin was so pale and thin that Nardole could make out the veins in her forehead.

'Please,' sniffed the girl. 'Let us in. I want my ma and da.' She wiped a tear from her eye and looked at Nardole pleadingly.

'What is she?' asked Nardole. 'Don't say she's a zombie! I don't like zombies.'

The Doctor tutted at Nardole and drew his sonic screwdriver from his jacket pocket. The girl watched impassively as he raised the device. Then he switched it on.

The girl's mouth opened sickeningly wide as she screamed. A screech of agony and primal rage, like a wounded animal. She fled to the stairwell, her gown drifting behind her, and as she reached the stairs she melted away, leaving behind a swirling cloud of mist.

The Doctor switched off the sonic and took a reading. 'Non-corporeal.'

'Non-what?' said Nardole.

'Didn't you notice when we were downstairs? She walked in out of the rain. She should've been drenched. Soaked to the skin.'

'She looked a *bit* damp.'

'Yes, but not damp *enough*. Because she wasn't really there. It's why she had to ask us to open the door, because she couldn't open it herself.'

'If she's a ghost, couldn't she just … walk through it? Some of them can do that, can't they?'

'Maybe she doesn't know that?' said the Doctor.

'Or fly. Sometimes they can fly.' A terrible thought occurred to Nardole. 'But she knew *we* were there. She talked to us!' He felt suddenly cold and hugged himself through his coat for warmth. 'Ugh! Shivers!'

The Doctor didn't reply. Instead, he returned to the door and knocked on it. 'Us again.'

Thomas opened the door and was visibly relieved to see there was no one but the Doctor and Nardole outside. 'You saw her? Our Catherine?'

'Yes,' said the Doctor, leading Nardole back into the warmth and light of the room. 'And now I know why you won't let her in.'

'She's a restless spirit,' said Isobel with a faraway look in her eyes. 'Lost between this world and the next.'

Nardole turned to the Doctor for explanation.

'Unshriven,' said the Doctor, with a face like a priest conducting a burial service. 'She died without making her final confession. Now her soul is in purgatory. "Doomed for a certain term to walk the night …"'

Bill warmed her hands on the bowl of soup. It seemed to be mostly cabbage and some other vegetables she couldn't identify, but at least it had been boiled so hopefully it wouldn't kill her. She took a sip, and it tasted of fish. She gave a thankful smile. 'Cheers for this.'

Betsy watched her eat, then fetched a bowl for herself. Agnes remained seated by the fire. She hadn't moved from the spot all evening.

'You not joining us?' asked Bill.

'I'm no' hungry,' said Agnes.

'Suit yourself. More for us, eh?'

'Dinnae mind her,' said Betsy. 'She's no' one for houseguests. Would prefer it if she was left alone, that one.'

'While you're happy to welcome in every passing stray,' said Agnes.

33

'Well, I'm glad you did,' said Bill. 'Owe you big time.' Betsy placed a flagon before her. It contained a cloudy brown liquid. 'What's this?'

'Ale.'

'You haven't got any water?'

'Why, are you wanting to make yersel sick?' said Betsy. 'Water, indeed!'

'Yeah,' said Bill. 'Poison, right?' She took a sip of the ale and immediately wished she had something else to wash her mouth out with. 'So … how long's all this been going on? This quarantine?'

'It's two months gone, since the first case,' said Betsy. 'And five weeks since they closed the gates.'

'Locking you all in with the plague?'

'Locking it *out*,' said Agnes sharply. 'If they hadnae closed the gates, we'd hae half of Leith bringing it intae the town.'

'That's how it's spread, is it?' said Bill. 'People?'

'Aye,' said Agnes. 'Through their foul air.'

'You mean their smell?' Bill finished her soup. She was pretty sure, if she remembered her history, that the plague was spread by fleas on rats. But she was also pretty sure she should keep that to herself. Not a good idea to tread on any butterflies.

'And their wickedness,' said Betsy. 'Let's no' forget, it is in the Lord's grace to spare those who remain faithful. This plague has been sent to test us.'

34

'Yeah,' said Bill. 'That's probably what it is. A test.'

'What about you?' said Agnes. 'You still havnae told us about yersel.'

'Not much to tell,' said Bill, taking another sip of the ale. For some reason, it didn't taste nearly as bad now. 'I travel about a bit, with a couple of friends.'

'Travel? And what do you dae? For work?'

'Well, I used to be a cook of sorts. I can fry a mean set of chips, let me tell you.' She paused. 'Only problem is, you haven't invented the potato yet.'

'These friends, they came wi' you here?' said Agnes, her manner softening. 'And left ye?' She sounded scandalised.

'I'll find them in the morning, I have a good idea where they'll be. We have a pre-arranged meeting place.' Bill paused. 'Assuming they haven't got themselves arrested.'

Agnes was appalled. 'These friends are other lassies like you?'

'God, no. No. More's the pity. No, it's a bloke called, well, who *likes* to be called the Doctor. And his friend, who is a sort of bodyguard, I suppose you'd call it. He looks out for him.'

'Two *men*?' If Agnes' eyes got any wider they would pop out of their sockets. 'And you travel wi' them?'

'Oh, no, it's nothing like *that*. I mean …' Bill leaned forward conspiratorially. 'Men are all right in short doses, but you wouldn't want to actually *live* with one, would you?'

Betsy gave a coughing, spluttering laugh from the corner. 'You may have a point there, pet.'

Agnes smiled at her, then caught herself smiling and corrected it with a frown. But Bill had seen it, though, and laughed.

'Now what might you be hee-hawing at, lassie?' said Agnes.

'You two!'

'What?'

'Don't worry. It's cool. I'm the same.'

'In what way?' said Betsy.

'I'm in no hurry to get married,' said Bill, choosing her words carefully. 'Who needs some great hairy man about the place, making the place untidy!'

'And there's the reek,' said Agnes. 'Dinnae forget about that!'

'And coming home all hours of the morning, blootered to high heaven!' said Betsy.

'Oh God, tell me about it!' laughed Bill. 'So how long have you been – how long have you lived together, you two?'

'I should say that is none of yer business—' said Agnes.

'Forty years,' said Betsy proudly, before adding, 'We keep each other company, is aw.'

I bet you do, thought Bill. I bet you do. Well, well, well! Even in Shakespeare times! 'I'm glad I ran into you two.' She looked into her flagon to see it was almost empty. She downed the remains in a single gulp. 'Cheers!'

Chapter

4

Bill groaned and opened her eyes, feeling like someone was banging a hammer inside her brain. Her left arm ached, as she had fallen asleep on top of it while twisted awkwardly in her chair. She was covered with a woollen blanket that felt and smelt like a stray dog. Betsy or Agnes must have draped it over her before going to bed. Bill couldn't remember saying goodnight to them, but the events of last night were all a little murky. She must have just fallen asleep.

Bill rubbed her left leg, just above the ankle, and it took a few seconds for her to notice why she was rubbing it. It itched, because of a sting. Or a bite. It was annoying, but not the end of the world.

There was a knock at the door leading to the bedroom, a polite cough, and Betsy entered, dressed in a smock with a tartan shawl. 'Ah. You're up.'

'Just about.' As Bill removed her blanket she felt the chill of the room. The fire in the grate was a pile of ashy logs. 'Sorry, must've dropped off.'

'You had a long day, I think,' said Betsy, pulling back two of the drapes to reveal a window, letting in some cold, bleak morning light.

Bill stood up and folded the blanket in a show of politeness before handing it to Betsy. 'It's hard to keep track, to be honest. Thanks again, for last night.'

'You're welcome. I'm sorry we cannae offer you breakfast, but …' Betsy's gaze indicated the shelves, which were empty save for some bowls and jugs.

'Oh God. I haven't eaten all your grub, have I?'

'Dinnae fash yersel, it's no trouble.'

'No, but … can I make it up to you?' Bill instinctively patted her pockets before she realised how ridiculous that was. But there would be money back in the TARDIS. Even if it wasn't the right currency for this era, there would be gold coins. The universal currency. 'Where do you buy your food?'

'It's brought in by the Netherbow Port at the bottom o' the High Street, there's a wee market. I'd normally go masel—'

'No need. I'll get you something,' said Bill. 'Least I can do.'

'Then haud on a while,' said Betsy, passing her a hooded cape. 'You'll want to wear this, if you dinnae want half the town's prying eyes.'

'If you're sure?'

'It belongs to Agnes, she'll no' miss it. She disnae like to leave the house.'

Bill pulled the cape on. It smelt like an old sack. 'Where is she, by the way?'

'Och, she's still in her pit, I dinnae like to wake her,' said Betsy with a smile. 'Now, away wi' you.'

'OK,' said Bill, heading for the door. 'I'll be back as soon as I can. And say thanks to Agnes when she wakes up. You two, you saved my life.' She lifted the hood of her cape, which was large enough to cover her hair and most of her face, if necessary. Then she opened the door and made her way downstairs.

Keeping the hood pulled close across her face, Bill retraced her route through the labyrinth of side streets. It was easy enough, as the alleyways were all slopes or steps, so she always chose the way upwards. The rain during the night had eased off, and had washed away the contents of the drains, and every now and then a gust of freezing, fresh air blasted Bill's eyes and nose.

She emerged onto the High Street. Even in full daylight it had a grim, desolate atmosphere, and was eerily deserted and silent. Bill felt like she was intruding, that she was being disrespectful just by being there.

The familiar stone edifice of the castle the Doctor had called 'the Heart of Midlothian' was to her right, meaning the side street leading to the TARDIS was nearby. She walked carefully back up the street, until she came to an alley she recognised, and hurried down the winding passages, slipping and half-tripping on the cobbles in her rush.

She turned a corner and, to her relief, the TARDIS stood ahead of her, just where they had left it. Some black mud and straw had gathered at its base. Bill approached it, wishing – not for the first time – that she had her own key. She knocked on the door as hard as she dared. 'Hello. Doctor?' There was no response. 'Nardole? Doctor? You in there?'

There was no reply. Bill gave the door a gentle push, but it refused to open. 'Come on. It's me, Bill Potts. You know me! Let us in!' She tried again and it failed to open, so finally she muttered the rudest word that sprang to mind and gave up, resting against the door while she thought what to do next. OK, the Doctor and Nardole weren't inside, so they were still around somewhere. Either they'd been captured by the guards, or they were looking for her. And if they were looking for her, they'd probably assume that *she* had been captured by the guards and be wherever the guards took their prisoners. Either way, there was only one thing to do.

Bill found her way back to the High Street and headed downhill. Within a few minutes, what she assumed was the Netherbow Port came into view. It was a large gatehouse, blocking the street and topped with a clock tower and spire. A group of women had gathered expectantly around the gate, baskets in hand, while soldiers kept watch. Like the soldiers she had seen yesterday, they were armed with staffs and had red crosses on their chests and backs. Then, just as Bill arrived, two soldiers opened the gate and hauled a cart loaded with cabbages and beans into the city. Whoever had brought the vegetables remained outside, while the two soldiers acted as shopkeepers, collecting payment and handing out vegetables. After a couple of minutes the cart was empty and the women were hurrying back to their homes, afraid of spending too much time in the company of potential plague carriers.

The soldiers counted out the money into one of the baskets on the cart, took some coins for themselves, then covered their faces with masks and dragged the cart outside. They returned inside before the farmer and his men approached their cart and hauled it away. Then they closed the gates.

'You've missed it,' said the soldier closest to Bill. 'Next load's in an hour.'

Bill thought she recognised the voice, and when she turned she saw it was one of the men who had pursued her the previous night. Presumably they worked long hours here or were very short staffed. But it being the same man made it easier.

Bill draw back her hood and grinned. 'Hiya.' The soldier's mouth fell open in amazement. 'Yeah. Curfew girl. Suppose you don't get many faces like mine around here.'

'The Barbary lass!' The soldier grabbed her by the wrist and called to one of his fellow guards. 'Rab! Take her to the Old Tolbooth. Let the Lord Provost decide what to dae wi' her.'

'Cheers,' said Bill, wincing at the soldier's grip. 'I was hoping you'd say that.'

The Old Tolbooth turned out to be the building that looked like a medieval castle. As the soldiers led Bill inside and an iron door closed behind her, it confirmed her suspicion that it was the town prison. Inside, she was taken up a winding staircase and pushed into a small, stone-walled cell. The straw on the floor gave it a horse-stable smell, and the dust in the air stung her eyes. Not that she could see much, as the only light was from a slit window high in the wall. Bill settled onto the bench and opened *Candy Crush Saga* on her phone.

After two hours, just as she was beginning to wonder if this hadn't been such a great plan after all, she heard the rumble of the bolt being drawn back in the lock. Outside was another soldier.

'The Lord Provost will see you now.'

The guard led her down a narrow passageway and into a large, wood-panelled room. Light poured in through the windows behind its occupant, a man seated at a desk. His face was in shadow, but Bill could make out a Guy Fawkes beard and shoulder-length hair. He wore a black doublet with long cuffs and a lace collar. As he saw her, he straightened his back and pinched the fingertips of his gloves.

'So this is our ... curfew-breaker?' he said. Bill guessed he was upper-class, as he selected his words carefully, like a lawyer.

'Sorry about that,' she said. 'Did you find the people I was with?'

'The people you were with?'

'Two men. A tall guy, grey hair, about sixty, and a little fat guy, bald.'

'No.'

'Oh,' said Bill.

'I'm sorry to disappoint you,' said the Provost dourly. 'Now. Do you want to explain what you are doing here?'

'We just arrived late last night, we didn't know about the quarantine.'

'By which port did you enter? I should like to have a word with the guards.'

'We didn't enter by a port ...'

'So you climbed o'er the Telfer wall? I thought as much. Come to rob the houses of the sick, nae doubt.'

'That's a bit of a leap, if you don't mind me saying.'

'It's a bit of a leap to climb o'er the wall,' said the Provost, smiling at his own joke. 'You're no' the first. And as you're clearly foreign to these shores, I assume a stowaway from a ship harboured in Leith and therefore a likely plague-carrier.'

'That's racist.'

'If I am mistaken, please correct me, and give a full account of yourself. Well?'

'Look, it's complicated, you wouldn't believe me.'

'Do you have any friends or relations in the town?'

Bill paused. 'No,' she said, not wanting to incriminate Betsy and Agnes.

'Then I have no choice. The penalty for breaking the quarantine, and concealing the plague, is to be taken and drowned in a quarry-hole.'

'I'm not concealing the plague,' said Bill. Her ankle chose that moment to itch, but more painfully.

The Provost cleared his throat, coughing into a handkerchief. 'Would you like us to check? I could send for the doctor?'

'You've gotta be kidding.'

'You wanted a doctor?' said a familiar voice from behind her.

Bill turned and felt a rush of relief. The Doctor was standing in the doorway, Nardole behind him. The Doctor jiggled his eyebrows and gave a manic grin.

'And who might you be, sir?' asked the Provost combatively.

The Doctor presented his psychic paper with a flourish. 'My credentials, sir.'

The Provost examined the wallet. 'The King's medical examiner ... Robert Louis Stevenson.'

'You *are* still loyal to the King, I presume?' said the Doctor, as though checking up on the Provost.

'Aye,' said the Provost. 'This town stands firm by his highness.'

'I'm very glad to hear it,' said the Doctor, holding out his hand for his wallet. The Provost returned it. 'And you are?'

'I, sir, am the Lord Provost, Sir John Smith.'

'Good name, very memorable,' said the Doctor. 'I take it you're in charge?'

'You are correct.'

'So you're responsible for the implementation of the anti-plague laws?'

'I am, sir.'

'So it's your idea to keep people prisoner in their own homes, under threat of death? To stigmatise the sick, as if they are responsible for their own misfortune? Sealing off entire households, just because one person is suspected – *suspected* – of being a plague-carrier?'

Smith glowered at the Doctor. 'I do what I must. To prevent the spread of the contagion. This is the worst outbreak this town has ever seen. Were it not for the plague laws there wouldn't be a single soul left alive.'

'Of course!' The Doctor grinned, then the grin faded. 'But some would say your laws are as great a public menace as the plague itself.'

'Really?' said Smith. 'Would you care to provide me with a list of their names and addresses?'

47

'How many have you needlessly sent to their deaths? How many have you condemned out of fear?' said the Doctor. 'Like my young friend here?'

'This … girl is known to you?'

'My maid,' said the Doctor casually. 'A rather headstrong girl, as I daresay you've noticed. Just after we entered your city, she decided to run away.'

'Yes, how *did* you get in without my knowledge—'

'That's a very boring question. I don't know, maybe your guards didn't inform you, they've got a lot on their mind. Does it matter? What matters is that you release my maid into my custody forthwith.'

'I see.' Smith turned to Bill. 'So this is why you were so interested to know if we'd found your two companions.'

'Yeah,' said Bill, playing along. 'Bang to rights.'

'And last night, your reason for breaking the curfew?'

The Doctor shrugged. 'We'd just caught up with her when your guards got in the way, like a bunch of idiots, and she ran off again.'

'You are willing to vouch for this … girl?' said Smith. 'You're quite certain she doesn't have the plague?'

'If she has, I will deal with her, in my own way.'

'If you insist. One less problem for me to deal with,' said Smith, taking a quill and scrawling a note on the scroll before him. 'I suggest you take better care of your servants in future, Doctor Stevenson.'

'And I suggest you take better care of your guards.' The Doctor turned to Bill. 'Come along. The Provost is a busy man, we've taken up enough of his time.'

Once they were safely in the corridor, Bill whispered, 'Thanks for that.'

'You're welcome,' the Doctor whispered back. 'When in doubt, get yourself captured, meet the fella in charge. Good plan!'

The Doctor led Bill and Nardole to the alleyway where the TARDIS had landed and bounded down the steps like an impatient gazelle.

'You saw a ghost? An actual, live ghost?' said Bill, following the Doctor down the steps.

'Well, I'm not sure "live" is quite the right term,' said Nardole. 'But certainly chatty.'

'Chatty? It spoke to you?'

'Oh yes. It was quite spooky, actually.'

'What about? What's it like to be dead?'

'We didn't get that far into the conversation,' said the Doctor, as they turned the corner and the TARDIS came into view. He rummaged in his jacket for his key and unlocked the door.

'Still,' said Bill. 'Pretty cool.' While the Doctor opened the TARDIS, she reached down and rubbed her ankle, twinging with the pain.

'Something wrong?' said the Doctor.

'Just an itch,' said Bill.

The Doctor scowled at her in concern, his eyes bulging. 'An itch?' He whipped out his sonic screwdriver and buzzed it at her.

'Hey, no need!'

The Doctor examined the screwdriver readout. 'Elevated antibodies. Bad news, Bill. You've got the plague.'

'What?' said Bill, following the Doctor into the TARDIS.

'The dreaded lurgi. You've got it,' said the Doctor, heading for the central control panel, his fingers twitching.

'Again, bedside manner needs work,' muttered Nardole, closing the door behind them.

Bill felt a flush of fear and nausea and anger. 'I've got the black death?'

'I shouldn't worry about it.' The Doctor adjusted a dial on the console which appeared to have no effect. 'TARDIS medical kit. Second roundel from the left, behind you.'

Bill turned and went down the short flight of steps to the corner of the console room. She pressed her hand against the glowing circle on the wall that was second from the left. 'How do I—'

As she spoke, the circle swung open to reveal a medicine cabinet plus a box of sticking plasters and a bandage roll.

'Bottle marked Fortified Streptomycin. Take one now, rest for six hours, you'll be right as rain.'

Bill found the jar, opened it, and took one pill, putting the jar in her pocket for safe keeping. 'That's all it takes? One pill?'

'One pill, yes,' said the Doctor. He circled the console, adjusting switches. 'The answer's no.'

'What?'

'To the question you're about to ask.'

'What question?'

'"If it's that easy, can't we help those poor people suffering outside?"'

'Seems a reasonable question.'

'It's an entirely unreasonable question.'

'Because it would mean changing history, right?'

The Doctor stared at Bill, wide-eyed, suddenly totally alien. 'Which is something we very much try not to do.' He cleared his throat. 'But …'

'But?'

'That's the next question. "But can't we save just one person. Surely one person won't make any difference?"'

'Yeah,' said Bill. 'And the reason we can't is …'

'If you save one person, you'll save another. Then ten. Then a hundred. Where would you stop? Where would you draw the line? *How* would you draw the line? You couldn't. Because if you do, it makes it *your* decision who lives or dies.'

'That's not a reason for not saving one person.'

'One person can change the world. No. Scrub that. *Every person* changes the world. Everybody affects the people around them, altering the course of events in a million chaotic ways. If one person lives who should die or dies who should live ... well, who knows what might happen.'

'But there's wriggle-room, right?' said Bill. 'There's always wriggle room.'

'Not today. Today is 1645, and this plague is one of the most awful in your planet's history. In this city it will cause untold grief, end thousands of lives – and we can't save a single one.'

'And on that cheerful note.' Nardole clapped his hands. 'Somewhere else?'

'Yes. Somewhere else,' nodded the Doctor, reaching for the dematerialisation lever.

'No,' said Bill, running up to the console. 'Not yet.'

'We can't stay here, Bill.'

'Those two old ladies who took me in. I owe them. I said I'd get them some food.'

The Doctor shrugged. 'They'll manage. Or they won't. That's history.'

'I promised. And I don't break my promises.'

'All right.' The Doctor raised his eyebrows devilishly. 'On one condition.'

'Which is?'

'You don't ask the question.'

'Fine. So, where do you keep the money?'

'Second wardrobe room, there's a chest, some gold sovereigns in there.'

'Cheers,' said Bill. She set off down the stairs, then halted. 'And anyway, haven't you got a mystery to solve?'

The Doctor sighed. 'Yes. We should leave. We definitely should leave.' His face broke into a wild grin, his eyes wide with excitement. 'But ... chatty ghosts!'

Chapter

5

'I'm not sure this is a good idea,' puffed Nardole, struggling to keep up with the Doctor's pace.

'Of course it's a good idea. I thought of it. Ergo, good.'

'What makes you think we'll see her again?'

The Doctor paused on the stairwell of the tenement, the same grim building they had visited the previous night. 'Because our friends said their daughter turned up every night, as regular as clockwork. Which is another odd thing. Ghosts are not generally known for their punctuality.'

Nardole shivered, tucking his hands into the pockets of his duffel coat. Night was already starting to fall and had brought with it a biting, cold wind. Looking up, beyond the looming hulk of the building, the cloudless sky was dotted with stars and a brilliant, white full moon. Somewhere up there, wondered Nardole, is somewhere warmer than where I am right now.

The Doctor unlocked the ground-floor door and crept inside like a thief, waving urgently for Nardole to follow.

'We'll leave the door open, make it easy for her,' whispered the Doctor, before bounding up the stairs.

Nardole hurried after him. At least in the moonlight he could see where he was going. When he reached the eighth floor, he paused to catch his breath and look out across the rolling slate rooftops of the city, the chimneys sending up ever-fading pillars of smoke. Beyond, he could even see the black shadow of the castle on the hill.

The Doctor knocked on the door. 'Me again.'

The door swung open and Isobel looked out. 'Thank the Lord you're here.'

'Yes!' said the Doctor. Then he realised what she'd said. 'What?'

Isobel wiped her eyes, then paused, the words difficult to say. 'It's Tam. He's sick.'

'Oh no.'

Nardole squeezed through the door after the Doctor. Inside, Thomas lay on a bed beside the fire, draped in a coarse blanket. He looked towards them with relief. His mouth was hanging open, sores around his lips, his skin ashen and soaked with sweat. 'Doctor …'

'Quiet.' The Doctor placed the back of his hand on Thomas's forehead.

'He came down wi' it right after you left,' Isobel explained. 'Can you do something? You said you were a doctor, after aw.'

'I am.' The Doctor carefully lowered the blanket to reveal Thomas's neck, and the tell-tale blotches below his ears. 'His immune system must've already been compromised for such a rapid deterioration.'

'But you can cure him, though?' said Isobel. 'Can you not?'

The Doctor looked to Nardole, his eyes full of agony.

Nardole gave him a sympathetic smile. 'I did say we should leave.'

'Hiya,' said Bill. 'Sorry I'm late.'

Betsy stood in the doorway, a bewildered look on her face. 'I didnae think you'd be back,' she said. 'I thought you might've given up on us.'

'Yeah, had a bit of a run-in with the law. All sorted now. Look.' Bill held up the basket in front of her. With the coins from the TARDIS, she had returned to the Netherbow gate and waited for the next cart to be brought in. The guard had got the memo that she was the King's examiner's maid, so they left her alone to buy as many fresh-looking vegetables as she liked, plus some logs for the fire. With the change, she picked up a loaf of bread on the way back from a baker's on the High Street. She got some fearful looks from the people of the city, but nobody wanted to get too close or make eye contact. Even a smile from her was enough to have people hurrying indoors.

Betsy inspected the contents of the basket with increasing delight. 'You got aw this?'

'Least I could do,' said Bill. 'So, are you gonna let me in or what?'

Betsy paused, as though unsure. 'You have naewhere else to be?'

'Not really.' The Doctor had given Bill a spare key for the TARDIS so she wouldn't end up stuck outside again, along with strict instructions to go to her room if she felt unwell. But she felt fine, and didn't fancy spending the night in the TARDIS waiting for the Doctor and Nardole to return from their ghost-hunting expedition. So she'd made the Doctor give her the address they were visiting with the intention of joining him later.

'I'd like to say hello to Agnes, if I may?' said Bill. 'Say thanks for the lend of her cape.'

'I'm afeart that'll no' be possible.'

Bill pulled the door shut behind her – she noticed it didn't have a lock – and followed Betsy up the stairwell.

'She's not still in bed?' asked Bill, as a joke.

'She's out, on a message. I'm expecting her home soon, though.'

Bill was about to remind Betsy that she'd said that Agnes didn't like leaving the house but thought better of it. Weird, though.

Betsy led Bill into the main room. She indicated the shelf lined with bowls and jugs. 'Up there.'

Bill nodded and started transferring the vegetables and bread to the shelf. It only took a few minutes. 'There you go.' She expected Betsy to say thank you, but no thanks came. Bill took off Agnes's cape and draped it over a chair. While she'd been in the TARDIS, she had taken the opportunity to pick up a black leather bomber jacket covered in patches for various space shuttle missions. It was a bit geeky but at least it would keep her warm.

'I suppose you'll be wanting fed,' said Betsy. She emptied a bowl of rainwater into a cauldron and propped it in the hearth. She then selected some logs and arranged them in the fireplace, then carefully brought the fire back to life with some dried leaves and gusts from the bellows.

'I'll keep an eye out for Agnes,' said Bill. She wandered over to the window, pulling back the thick black drapes, and looked down into the small square.

There were seven people standing in the square, caught in the silver moonlight. They hadn't been there a minute ago when Bill had knocked on Betsy's door. She couldn't make out their faces, but from their clothing she guessed it was two men, four women, and a small girl with thick, curly hair, standing barefoot on the cobbles. They were all dressed in their normal working clothes: squared-off coats for the men, heavy dresses for the women, save for the child who wore a loose-fitting nightgown, oblivious to the cold even as the wind snapped at the thin material. The strangest thing, though, was that they were all standing perfectly still, all facing in the same direction, their arms by their sides. Motionless and silent. They were waiting.

'Oh my God,' said Bill under her breath.

Then the little girl looked up at her. With lifeless, doll-like eyes and a vengeful scowl. She would have been quite pretty, but her cheeks were hollow and her lips were a dark blue. Her skin was as pale and shiny as candle wax.

Bill shivered, a chill running down her spine like the memory of a half-forgotten nightmare. Then the little girl turned her gaze to face directly in front of her, and she walked. The other six ghosts began to move, striding forward in perfect unison, measuring out each pace. One of them walked to the doorway of the house opposite while the other six, including the girl, made for the alleyway leading to the High Street.

'What d'you think you're doing?' snapped Betsy, pulling Bill away from the window. She drew the drapes across it. 'Letting the heat out.'

'Sorry,' mumbled Bill. 'Didn't you see—'

'No, and neither did you,' said Betsy emphatically. 'Best left alone.'

'I should go,' said Bill, twisting herself free of Betsy's grip. She ran to the door, swinging it shut behind her, and hurried down the stairs, gripping the wooden banister.

The stairs twisted sharply. Bill turned the corner to see a figure coming up the stairs. The figure moved into a sliver of moonlight through a window – and it was Agnes. She looked up at Bill, as she slowly continued up the stairs. She smiled. 'It's Bill, is it no'?'

'Yeah,' said Bill. 'Where've you been?'

Agnes frowned, as though she didn't understand the question. She walked up another step, then stopped.

'I didn't see you outside,' said Bill. 'How did you get past the ghosts?'

'Ghosts?' said Agnes with a dry chuckle. Another step. 'I've seen nae ghosts. The very notion!'

'Sorry, don't have time for this, gotta go,' said Bill. She hurried down the stairs and Agnes moved aside to let her past. Bill hurried past her, then reached the door which was hanging wide open and letting in a blast of freezing air. Agnes must've left it open, she thought, as she emerged onto the square.

Bill looked around. The door of the house opposite was shut, and all the windows were in darkness. She hurried over to the alleyway leading to the High Street – and as she turned the corner, she saw the little girl hesitating in a shaft of moonlight. The girl laughed and skipped away into the darkness, as though playing a game.

Bill reached into her pocket, pulled out a torch, switched it on and gave chase.

The Doctor rummaged through the jars, picking them up, sniffing them, wincing and discarding them.

'What you looking for?' asked Isobel.

'Meadowsweet,' said the Doctor. 'Do you have any?'

Isobel reached past him for a wooden bowl containing what looked to Nardole like a pile of dried flowers and twigs. 'Here.'

The Doctor sniffed it. 'Good. Boil up some water, let's make some tea.'

Isobel nodded and filled the cauldron. While she was busy, Nardole edged up to the Doctor. 'Salicylic acid?'

'The best we can do,' the Doctor whispered back. 'Should reduce the fever.'

Nardole sucked his teeth. 'Not going to cure him, though, is it?'

'We can't,' said the Doctor under his breath. 'Because if we saved one …'

'We'd have to save them all?' Nardole looked across at Thomas. He was sleeping, his chest rising and falling as he drew in weak, croaking breaths. The lumps on his neck had spread with astonishing speed.

'We can make sure he doesn't suffer,' said the Doctor. 'That's all we can do.'

'What are you two chuntering on about?' said Isobel as she fixed the cauldron over the fire. 'Thick as thieves!'

'Just discussing treatment.' The Doctor took the bowl of meadowsweet and tipped it into a tankard. 'Once the water's boiled, pour it in here—'

He was interrupted by a voice coming from outside. The voice of a young woman. 'Let us in. Please. Dinnae leave us out here in the dark.'

Isobel froze. Nardole turned to the Doctor, who was listening intently. He put up a finger to shush Nardole.

'Let us in, please. I want my ma and da,' said the girl from outside.

The Doctor crept across the room to the door.

'You cannae let her in,' said Isobel. 'She's deid! Her soul is forsaken!'

The Doctor reached for the door. 'Isobel, it might be a good idea for you to wait in the other room.'

Nardole gave Isobel his most reassuring smile. 'The Doctor knows what he's doing,' he told her. 'You have nothing to worry about.'

'How do ye ken that?' said Isobel.

'I've known the Doctor for over twenty years. He's saved my life, ooh, at least three times. You can trust him.'

Isobel looked at the Doctor. He smiled at her apologetically. She checked on her sleeping husband, tucking his blankets into place, then, with one last, fearful glance towards the door, she withdrew to her bedroom.

'Let us in,' said the girl from outside, her plea becoming a wail. 'Please.'

The Doctor took a deep breath, then pulled the door open. He stepped aside and gestured for the person outside to come in.

Nardole backed against the wall as the young woman walked into the room, looking around slowly, taking in her surroundings with a lopsided smile. She was exactly as he had seen her yesterday; the same long, cotton nightdress, the same porcelain-white skin. She had so little colour about her, it was like she had stepped out of an old black-and-white photograph.

Thomas groaned and his straw bed rustled as he shifted in his sleep. Catherine turned towards him with a look of concern. 'Da? What's happened?'

The Doctor closed the door and darted around to place himself between the girl and her father. 'He's not feeling very well.'

Startled, Catherine gave a series of short gasps. 'What's wrong wi' him?'

'I think you know,' said the Doctor. 'The same thing that happened to you.'

The girl's face crumpled, overcome by the pain. 'The plague? No.' Then she glared at the Doctor accusingly. '*Who are you?*'

'You don't remember me? We met yesterday, on the stair.'

'I remember.' The girl acknowledged Nardole with wry amusement. 'You were there too. But what are you doing in my home? An' where's my ma?'

'She's … not here right now,' said the Doctor hurriedly. Nardole winced, very conscious that Isobel would be able to hear everything from the bedroom. 'But she's alive,' the Doctor continued. 'As to who we were. I'm the Doctor, this is my friend Nardole –' Nardole gave Catherine a cheery wave – 'and we're here to help.'

'To help?'

'Like yesterday, when we helped you into the building,' said the Doctor. 'Tell me, what were you doing outside?'

Catherine frowned. 'I … dinnae ken,' she said distantly. 'I dinnae remember going out … There's a curfew …'

'No, but you remember us, which is interesting,' said the Doctor. 'And after we saw you, where did you go?'

'I …' Catherine fell silent with a shake of her head.

'She doesn't remember disappearing?' whispered Nardole to the Doctor.

The Doctor indicated for Nardole to remain quiet. 'Catherine. You had the plague. Do you remember that?'

'Aye,' said Catherine. 'I remember … suddenly feelin' sae wabbit, sae hot, so I went off to bed. And ma brought me water and sat aside my bed, and kept the fire going …' She trailed off, puzzled.

'And after that?' said the Doctor. 'What do you remember after that?'

Catherine shook her head and laughed. 'Nothin'. Was only yesterday ...'

'That was over a week ago,' said the Doctor. 'Where have you been in the meantime?'

'Naewhere,' said Catherine. 'I've no' been anyplace, was only yesterday.'

'You don't remember being visited by the Night Doctor? You don't remember him taking you away?'

'No.' Catherine's eyes widened with terror. 'I wasnae visited by him ... If I was ... I'd be ...'

'Yes,' said the Doctor regretfully. 'I'm very sorry, there's no easy way of saying this, but you're dead.'

'No,' said Catherine with an incredulous laugh. 'I cannae be!'

'You think you got better? But you know that once somebody's got the plague, they *never* get better, do they?'

Catherine didn't reply. She turned to face the fire, her tear-stained cheeks glistening in the flame light, her chest heaving with impotent anger. In the fireplace, the cauldron started to boil.

'How do you feel?' said the Doctor. 'Do you still feel sick?'

Catherine shook her head. 'I cannae be deid. I remember ... dancing, I remember running o'er the fields, picking berries in the sunshine ...'

'I'm sure you have a full set of memories,' said the Doctor. 'Of everything but your own death. Because the copy was made before you died. When you were on your deathbed ...'

'The copy?' said Catherine.

'That's what you are, I'm afraid. You're not Catherine, you're ... an echo. An after-image.'

'A ghost,' added Nardole helpfully. 'That's why you couldn't open the doors – though you could try passing through them ...'

'A *ghost*?' Catherine's face filled with horror. She looked down at her bare, white arms, pressing the pallid flesh. 'I'm a ghost?'

The Doctor reached out a hand, palm-forward. 'Try touching my hand.'

'No.' Catherine protested.

'Try.'

'No, I winnae!' Catherine shook her head and glanced at the door, looking for a way out.

The Doctor pulled out his sonic screwdriver and buzzed it at her before checking the reading. 'You're a psychic projection. A perfect recreation of Catherine, with all her hopes, dreams and memories – and the capacity to gain new ones, which is particularly cruel – but you're not her. You're not alive.'

Catherine rubbed her eyes to hold back the tears, and headed for the door. Then she halted, realising that she would be unable to open it.

'You see,' said the Doctor. 'Non-corporeal. I'm very sorry.'

'No,' sobbed Catherine. 'No. I'm no' … I'm no' …' She covered her head with her hands – and, to Nardole's astonishment, he could see the black shape of the door behind her. She was fading away, becoming as transparent as a reflection on glass, her feet and legs already a swirl of mist. 'I'm no' deid!' she cried imploringly, before melting away like breath on a cold day.

After a moment, the Doctor called out 'It's all right. She's gone.'

Isobel appeared at the bedroom door, her eyes red, her cheeks stained with tears. 'She didnae ken,' said Isobel weakly. 'She didnae ken she was deid!'

'Yes,' said the Doctor with quiet determination. 'Whatever's doing this, whatever's brought her back, it has to end. Let you grieve in peace.'

Chapter

6

It was as if the city had come to life at night. Bill halted in the alleyway, her heart pounding, looking out onto the High Street, the flagstones shining in the misty moonlight. There were, she guessed, over five hundred ghosts on the street, all walking slowly to their destinations. They looked solid and could almost be real people, were it not for their mortuary-slab faces, their heavily shadowed eyes, their sunken cheeks and exposed teeth, and the black blisters and boils of the plague. There were all ages: men with bald heads, woman with white wisps of hair, middle-aged, bearded labourers and shop-workers and housewives in smocks, and young people of 19, 20. But all stick-thin, with lurching gaits and arched backs, signs of the starvation that had left them vulnerable to the disease. There were even families: couples walking through the moonlight hand-in-hand, parents leading their children. And the ghosts were aware of each others' presence. As they passed on the way, men would nod and lift their hats, women would bow, exchanging a few silent words of greeting.

Because that was the other striking thing. The only sound was Bill's breath, as she recovered from chasing the small girl up the alleyway. None of the ghosts made a noise, not a word, not a footstep. She watched as one man with a fine-looking long-coat strutted by, walking through a puddle without disturbing the surface. It was like they were three dimensional-images projected not on a screen but into the air. Holograms?

Bill didn't feel frightened. She felt strangely calm and detached, like drifting off to sleep. The ghosts didn't seem to be aware of her presence. The little girl she had followed had disappeared into the crowd, darting between the legs of the adults, until Bill couldn't follow her any more.

One of the ghosts, a stern-looking woman with large eyes like overripe fruit suddenly turned towards Bill. Bill shuddered and pressed herself against the wall – and the ghost walked straight past, down the passageway, completely oblivious. Bill let out a deep breath of relief, and tentatively walked out into the street. She made sure to keep her distance from the ghosts, not wanting to draw attention to herself, not wanting to do that whole ghost-walks-through-you thing. They were ghosts, they could do that; she could take that as read. Instead, she approached the Old Tolbooth, keeping to one side of the street.

A crowd of ghosts had gathered around an unremarkable alleyway opposite the prison. They seemed to be waiting their turn to enter the side street, as the entrance was only wide enough to allow two people to enter at once. Bill approached cautiously, and as she drew closer she saw that inside the alleyway the ground dropped away into total blackness.

Bill waited until all the ghosts had disappeared into the darkness, then approached the alleyway, keeping her torchlight trained on the ground in front of her. She raised the torch beam up the side of the passageway, where it picked out a rudimentary street sign.

Mary King's Close.

Keeping the torchlight trained on the steps, Bill slowly made her way down. She didn't quite know why, but it was as if something had drawn her to this place. As though the blackness were sucking her in. And once again she got the strange shiver of déjà vu, as though this was a moment from a long-forgotten nightmare.

What was that smell? It was a familiar, chemistry lab smell. Like rotten eggs. Her torchlight picked out a drifting fog and Bill felt the insides of her nostrils begin to sting. She breathed through her mouth, and it stung her throat, a dry, burning sensation. And that was the other strange thing – the air here was *warm*, like standing outside a Gregg's on a winter's day.

She reached the bottom of the steps, where the street continued ahead of her, winding ever downward into the impenetrable dark. Even her torchlight had no effect on the blackness. The street remained narrow, no wider than two metres. Above her the street was criss-crossed with lines from which hung grey sheets like sleeping bats, blocking off any view of the upper levels, turning the alleyway into a tunnel. It was like she was descending into a cave.

Somewhere ahead of her a child was crying while its mother sang a slow, mournful lullaby. And then there was raucous laughter, and chatter, and shouts of anger, a woman bawling: 'Get out! You were a drunkard and wastrel when ye were alive, Joe Lowry! Now you're deid, won't ye leave us be, an' get yersel to Hell where you belong!'

Bill's torch suddenly revealed a crowd of ghosts in a square surrounded by wooden-beamed houses. There were so many, packed so tightly, it was like the overspill of a heaving inn. Ghosts of gnarled, pinch-faced old men and women sat on the doorsteps, trading malicious gossip. Ghosts of broken-nosed, burly men prowled the balconies, fuming at those inside the houses to let them in. 'Open the door, ye besom! Or I'll drag ye down wae me!' And the ghosts of young women wandered aimlessly through the throng, their faces blank with horror, bundles of rags clutched to their breasts.

Bill felt an ache in her chest at the misery of it all. The pity. The ghosts, desperate to return to their loved ones, couldn't understand why they were being turned away.

And their loved ones were probably huddling in terror in the darkness, holding their children close, hoping that these apparitions of cruel husbands, unfaithful wives and spiteful elderly relations would leave them alone. It was a vision of utter wretchedness, as though all the anguish, the bitterness and heartbreak was a physical force, a black wall pushing her away.

The little girl that Bill had followed was there. As she was picked out in Bill's torchlight, she turned to face Bill, staring directly into the beam. Her eyes were the colour of sour milk, her skin hideously pale, her lips black. She opened her mouth and screamed, a howl of pure hatred. The loathing of the dead for the living. Then the other ghosts turned towards Bill, and opened their mouths to reveal black, toothless holes.

Bill felt a sudden blast of hot air against her face, making her skin prickle, like looking into an open oven. Her throat gagged at the acrid stench. The ghosts then joined in with the little girl's scream, some howling, others moaning, others cursing. And they started to walk slowly up the street towards her, their eyes burning with anger.

Her stomach churning, Bill retreated, turned, and ran up the street as quickly as she could.

Thomas groaned and coughed, his whole chest convulsing with the effort. Isobel cradled his head, stroking his beard. 'He's getting worse.'

'Yes,' said the Doctor grimly, staring into space, a man haunted by time. 'I'm sorry.' Four hours had passed since Catherine's visit and now it was, by Nardole's estimation, three o'clock in the morning. The Doctor didn't need to sleep – he liked to say it was for tortoises – but Nardole's eyes were weighing heavily, and he kept jerking awake each time he started sliding out of his chair.

Isobel loosened her husband's nightshirt, revealing more painful sores. The meadowsweet tea had alleviated Thomas's fever and sent him to sleep, but it hadn't halted the progression of the disease. His fingertips and lips were already turning purple. Sooner or later, his body would give up the fight. 'It's just like with our Catherine,' said Isobel. 'It's sae quick. Is there nae mair you can do?'

Nardole gave the Doctor a look as though to say 'Go on, just this once', and the Doctor shook his head. 'I've done everything I can,' he said.

'He's gonnae die?' said Isobel, struggling to get the words out. 'I'm going tae lose him too?'

'Not yet,' said the Doctor. 'There's something that has to happen first.'

Isobel looked at him uncomprehendingly. 'What?'

There were four slow, heavy thuds against the door. The Doctor held his breath, holding up a hand for silence, his eyes alert.

Isobel recoiled in horror, her eyes filling with tears. 'No ... No!'

'Statement. Anyone visited by the Night Doctor will soon die,' said the Doctor. 'Conjecture. Nobody can die without being visited by the Night Doctor first!'

'I'm not sure that's entirely logical,' muttered Nardole.

'Call it an educated guess,' said the Doctor, then froze as there were four more heavy thuds at the door. 'Which turned out to be correct. The Night Doctor knows who is going to die and makes it his business to call on them just before they draw their last breath. Why? And how does he know who is at death's door?'

'Well, there's one way to find out,' said Nardole, with a meaningful raise of his eyebrows.

'Yes,' said the Doctor. 'Ask him.'

'You were hoping he'd come here!' snapped Isobel. 'That's why you kept on!'

'I was testing a hypothesis,' said the Doctor grimly. 'Which I'd hoped would be wrong.' He approached the door, then waited until there were four more knocks.

'You cannae let him in,' said Isobel with a sob. 'Please ...'

The Doctor opened the door suddenly, then hurried into the room to stand back against the far wall, as if he had lit a firework. Nardole edged alongside him, keeping a careful watch on the black, empty doorway. Isobel stared at it too, with a desperate, terrified look in her eyes.

A figure in a long cloak stooped to pass through the doorway, then straightened up to its full height, its head nearly touching the ceiling beams. It looked from side to side, taking in the room through its welder's goggles eyes, peering at each of the occupants down its long, curved beak. Seeing Thomas, it proceeded towards the bed without the sound of a footstep, the only noise the slither of its animal-hide robe against the floor. As it got closer, Nardole was suddenly overwhelmed by the stench of decomposing herbs and flowers, like someone had sprayed air freshener over a sewage leak. Trying not to sneeze, Nardole wafted the air in front of his nose. 'Pooh!'

The Doctor placed himself between the Night Doctor and Thomas. 'Hello. I'm the Doctor.'

The figure halted, as though surprised. Then it motioned with its right hand. Or rather, with its leathery, long-nailed glove. In its other glove, Nardole noticed, it held a long staff of roughly finished iron, with a sharpened point at the end.

As the figure didn't reply, the Doctor continued. 'You must be the Night Doctor. I've heard a lot about you, but I've got questions. How do you know when people are about to die?'

The figure reached out a claw and shoved the Doctor aside. The Doctor, startled, fell against Nardole. The Night Doctor then pulled back the blanket covering Thomas and raised the end of its staff to point at the sleeping man's chest.

'Ah, I thought as much,' said the Doctor. 'You're the one making the copies. You pop in at the last possible moment to perform a scan of their body and mind, yes? Then you upload them somewhere and they're resurrected, after a fashion, as psychic projections, with the capacity to interact and learn – but blissfully non-cognisant of their own insubstantiality. Am I right?'

The Night Doctor slowly drew the staff along the length of Thomas's body, as though making a surgical incision in the air, then let it hover over his forehead.

'Don't leap in with an answer,' said the Doctor. 'I know I'm right. That staff of yours is a dead giveaway. It's not of this planet or this time. Some sort of energy-wave interferometer, I expect. Although that is something I've just made up, so maybe not.'

The Night Doctor lifted the end of its staff from Thomas's forehead and turned to depart.

'No, wait,' said the Doctor, darting around to block its way. 'You still haven't told me *why* you're doing this. Why are you making ghosts? Who are you working for? You can tell me. I'm a Doctor too, a fellow practitioner, I have a professional interest.'

The Night Doctor drew itself up to its full height and stared at the Doctor impassively with its glassy eyes. Then it raised its free hand and gestured for him to move out of its way.

'And the most important question of all,' said the Doctor. 'What exactly is under that mask of yours ...'

The Doctor leaned forward, gripped the end of the Night Doctor's beak, and squinted deep into its eye sockets. 'Oh no,' he breathed. 'Oh no.'

'What is it?' said Nardole.

'Nothing,' said the Doctor. 'There's nothing under there, nothing at all ...'

The Night Doctor raised its free hand – and there was a sudden howl of freezing wind which sent the Doctor sprawling across the floor. Then the wind ceased, and the Night Doctor glided over to the door, opened it, and ducked down to leave.

'No, wait!' said the Doctor, pulling himself to his feet. He rummaged in one of his pockets, then ran over to examine Thomas, placing his hand over the sleeping man's mouth. Then he hurried over to Isobel, who was rigid with shock. He held his hands to her cheeks and looked deep in her eyes. 'Keep him warm, plenty to drink, only boiled water, more meadowsweet tea.' Isobel nodded and the Doctor released her. 'Nardole?'

'Yes?' said Nardole.

'Stay here, keep an eye on things.' That said, the Doctor ran out of the door, slamming it behind him.

Nardole patted his hands together and gave Isobel an apologetic look. 'Sorry. He does that.'

* * *

The Doctor piled down the stairs, using the walls to steady himself in the absence of any banisters. The stairwell was precipitous and treacherous, but fortunately the moonlight – and his keen eyesight – meant he could see where he was going, just about. He jumped the last few steps to the landing of the fourth floor, which was empty. He should have caught up with the Night Doctor by now. The fellow wasn't moving that quickly. So where was he?

Acting on a hunch, the Doctor hurried over to the window and looked down into the street. And there was the Night Doctor, emerging from the door on the ground floor, its beak clearly visible from beneath its wide-brimmed hat. It then began to glide up the street with surprising speed, as though it was floating.

Which, thought the Doctor, it probably was. There was nothing beneath that cloak but thin air. When he'd looked into its eyes all he had seen was a hollow space, an empty darkness where a face should be. There were no arms inside the sleeves, no hands inside the gloves. Something must be controlling it, animating the outfit, guiding it by remote control. The same something that was creating the psychic projections? It seemed a reasonable inference, but that only raised more questions.

A mystery! With a rush of exhilaration, the Doctor bounded down the next set of stairs. He turned the corner, rushed down the next stairwell, then the next, until he emerged onto the street, just in time to see the Night Doctor drifting away, a gap of several centimetres between the bottom of its robe and the cobbles. He was right – it could levitate! After all, with no feet, it would have nothing to keep on the ground.

The Night Doctor floated into the alleyway that led to the cathedral and the High Street. The Doctor sprinted after it, his feet twisting on the uneven ground, his breath freezing in the air. He turned the corner where he had last seen the Night Doctor and stared up the street; the houses to his left, the brooding hulk of the cathedral to his right.

The street was empty. The Doctor circled on the spot, searching the forlorn-looking windows and the boarded-up doors, some marked with crosses. Every house appeared to have been abandoned. Maybe the Night Doctor had accelerated, and was on the High Street somewhere?

A heavy flapping sound came from above, like a tarpaulin whipping in the wind. Or a set of leathery wings. The Doctor looked up, past the stained-glass windows of the cathedral, past the turrets, until his gaze reached the ornate stone spire in the shape of a crown. And there, standing on the edge of the parapet, silhouetted against the sky, was the distinctive shape of the Night Doctor, gazing out over the city.

The sound of approaching footsteps made the Doctor look down, but not soon enough, as Bill hurtled into his chest, nearly knocking him off his feet. He steadied her.

She was panting, as though she'd been running for dear life. 'Bill?'

Bill took in a big gulp of air. 'Doctor!' she sighed with relief. 'Thank God.'

'What happened?' said the Doctor. He couldn't help glancing back at the spire, but the Night Doctor had disappeared. 'Are you all right?'

'Fine, I just … had a bit of a run-in with some ghosts. Accidentally gate-crashed their party.'

'Were there high spirits?' said the Doctor.

Bill laughed despite herself, then pouted at him in mock indignation. 'I'm serious. It was well scary. What are you doing out?'

'Trying to get an appointment with the Night Doctor,' said the Doctor. 'But he had to fly.'

'What was that?'

'A figure of speech—' began the Doctor.

'No, not that,' said Bill, her eyes darting around fearfully. She waved her torch around the street, up the walls of the nearest house. 'I heard something. Like a blocked drain …'

The Doctor looked around. There was nothing out of the ordinary, but Bill was right. There was a *presence*. And a sound. A rhythmic squelching, like listening to someone's stomach with a stethoscope. And a sporadic slithering, like something was laboriously dragging itself across the ground towards them.

'You can hear it?' whispered Bill.

'I can,' said the Doctor. 'And it's not a blocked drain—'

'Doctor, watch out!' cried Bill.

The Doctor whirled around to see what she was warning him about. There was something on the ground, a black, gelatinous shape, like a sliding shadow. It scurried towards him like a hungry rat and launched itself at him through the air. It thumped against his midriff, winding him in the stomach, and he felt teeth or claws scratching through his waistcoat and into his flesh. His last impression was of the creature's stench: the clammy, musty smell of abandoned tombs and graveyards. The pain in his stomach increased, and he heard Bill shouting. Then he stumbled backwards into a deep, cold nothingness.

Chapter

7

The Doctor groaned and opened one of his eyes. He looked left and right suspiciously, then sat bolt upright. 'What happened?'

Bill looked at Nardole, who indicated for her to do the talking. 'Something attacked you in the street. It was like a rat, or a dog.'

'Like a rat or a dog, but not a rat or not of dog. I remember that.' The Doctor pulled the blanket from over his legs and climbed out of the bed. 'It's what happened while I was knocked unconscious I'm a little less sure about.'

'Yeah, you were dead to the world,' said Bill, warming her fingers by the fireplace. 'And I gave the whatever-it-was a right slap. I must've hurt it, because the next thing I knew, it'd done a runner.'

'You didn't get a good look at it?'

'No, I was too busy being worried about you.'

The Doctor prowled around the room, stretching his legs. 'And then?'

'Well, I couldn't leave you lying in the gutter. So I ran here, to get Nardole. And he helped me drag you back here, because it was closer than the TARDIS.'

'Eight flights of stairs,' said Nardole. 'Can I just repeat that for emphasis? Eight flights. Of stairs.'

'And Isobel was kind enough to take you in, and set up a bed.'

'Isobel? And Thomas? Where are they?'

There was a cough from the doorway leading to the bedroom. Isobel stood there, Thomas beside her. He looked pale and weak and his skin was still mottled with sores but he looked vastly better than he'd been when Bill had brought in the Doctor. His fever had faded and he could breathe without groaning.

'Thomas!' said the Doctor. 'You're looking ... well.'

Thomas nodded. 'Aye. And feeling it.'

'Turns out, not awbody does die after a visit frae the Night Doctor,' said Isobel, smiling affectionately at her husband.

'No,' said the Doctor. 'Perhaps this Night Doctor isn't infallible after all.'

'Um, Doctor,' said Bill. 'Can I have a word? In private?'

'I don't see why not.'

'I'll get you something to eat,' said Isobel, attending to the hob. 'After being asleep half the morn, you'll be wanting some breakfast.'

'Least we can dae,' added Thomas, sitting down on the vacated bed.

Bill led the Doctor into the Abneys' bedroom. It was dark, barely larger than the bed, and stank of straw. Bill sat on the bed and prepared for the lecture that would follow. 'I know you said it was against the rules ...'

'You gave Thomas one of the pills from the TARDIS,' said the Doctor, gently closing the door behind them.

'Yes,' admitted Bill. 'I'm sorry.'

'You're sorry? After everything I told you about not altering the course of history? How we can't save anyone, not even one man. How, as travellers in the fourth dimension, we have a unique responsibility—'

'I know all that,' said Bill. 'But I could hardly stand by and watch him die, could I?'

'So you decided to take matters into your own hands, and hang the consequences?'

'I had to do it. Maybe I'm not cut out for this, if it's a problem for you.'

'You didn't *have* to do it,' the Doctor reminded her.

'No, I *did*. I'm not like you, I can't just stand back and go, "Ooh, it's the course of established history." I'm sorry, but I care what happens to people.'

'No,' said the Doctor. 'I mean, you didn't have to do it. Because I'd already given him one of the pills last night.'

'What?'

'Just before I left.' The Doctor stared at her with mock indignation. 'What, you think I could leave him to die?'

'You mean, he would've got better anyway?'

'He was already *getting* better. If I hadn't given him the pill when I did, he wouldn't have lasted the night.'

'So now he's had two pills? Is that gonna be a problem?'

'No,' said the Doctor. 'If anything, it'll hasten the effect. And give him a great complexion.'

'So all that stuff about how we can't save even a single person—'

'Is undeniably and incontrovertibly true,' said the Doctor. 'But I admit there is a fractional degree of wriggle-room …'

'I knew it!'

'But now we have to draw the line.'

'At saving one man.'

'Right.'

'But if we can save one—'

'No,' said the Doctor. 'You're not going to ask that question. One life, we just might be able to get away with, if we're lucky. But this has to be it.'

Bill sighed. 'How come it's OK for you to make these decisions, and not me?'

'Because I'm a Time Lord. That makes it my call. My pay grade.'

'You're pulling rank on me?' said Bill. The Doctor pulled an expression of such offence that she couldn't help but laugh. 'All right, you're a "Time Lord". I get that. But why did you leave it to the last minute to give Thomas the tablet? And why didn't you tell Nardole?'

'Because,' said Nardole, creeping in to join them, 'Thomas had to be genuinely close to death in order for the Night Doctor to come.'

'Yeah,' said the Doctor. 'It was a bit touch and go for a minute there, I'll admit …'

'So who is this "Night Doctor"?' asked Bill.

'Ah. That's the thing. We have another …' Nardole mouthed 'visitor'.

Bill followed the Doctor back into the main room and recoiled in shock at the figure standing by the door. A figure dressed in a long, black robe with a wide-brimmed hat and a bird's skull mask. It stooped as it entered, as though in deference.

'He's come back,' whispered Nardole, rather unnecessarily.

The masked figure walked to the centre of the room, its boots clumping on the floorboards.

'Oh, no!' said the Doctor. 'It's day. This must be the Day Doctor!' He welcomed the figure with a wild grin. 'Hello!'

'Where is the one with the plague?' growled the figure, its voice muffled by the bird mask.

'You see,' said the Doctor to Nardole. 'Much more chatty!' He turned back to the plague doctor. 'Who told you there was someone with the plague here?'

The figure stared at him with its looking-glass eyes. 'It is my business to know.'

'It wasn't you, Isobel?' asked the Doctor. Isobel shook her head. 'Thomas?' Thomas gave a negative shrug. 'No, sorry,' said the Doctor. 'Must've been one of the neighbours. Old Jack McCavity, what is he like! You shouldn't believe gossip. Nobody with the plague here.'

The figure indicated Thomas. 'I was told that Thomas Abney was sick.'

'He was sick, yes,' said the Doctor. 'Spot of food poisoning. Ate some bad oats. But as you can see, he's up and about now. Aren't you, Thomas?'

Thomas nodded. 'I'm fine now, all good.'

'So …' The Doctor was now so close to the masked figure that he was staring right into its eyes. 'There's no risk of infection. You can take the mask off now. Don't worry. Your secret is safe with us.'

'Who are you?' said the figure gruffly.

'Me?' The Doctor backed away with a flourish. 'I'm the Doctor.'

'Doctor Robert Louis Stevenson,' Nardole added helpfully.

'The King's medical examiner,' added Bill.

The masked figure stared at the Doctor for several seconds, then reached up and pulled off its wide-brimmed hat and drew back its hood. Then it lifted its mask to reveal the face of a woman in her forties with long, curly red hair, her face wet with perspiration. She had high cheekbones and a strong jawline, putting Bill in mind of Katherine Hepburn. The woman brushed away some hairs stuck to her forehead and reached out a hand for the Doctor to shake – then, realising she was still wearing a heavy glove, she removed it.

'The Doctor? Thank goodness,' she said, in a husky voice. 'I've been looking for ye everywhere. My name's Annabelle Rae. Will ye come with me?'

Her face concealed with the mask, Annabelle led them through the streets to her home on the edge of the city. Her house resembled a miniature manor with an attached tower, and even had a herb garden with some tangled bushes growing in the shadow of the city walls. Once the Doctor, Bill and Nardole were inside, she locked and bolted the door behind them and hung the key from a nail. Then she removed her hat, mask and gloves and placed them on wall hooks.

Finally, she lifted back her hood and ruffled her hair. 'I cannot be seen wearing the plague doctor's attire,' she said, in reply to the obvious question. 'The people are not to know who I am.'

'Cos you're a woman?' guessed Bill.

'Because I am not my father, Doctor George Rae,' said Annabelle. She unfastened her cloak and hung it from the remaining free hook. 'They must believe he still lives, that *he* is still the plague doctor.'

'Why, what happened to—' Bill stopped herself as she guessed the answer.

'Quite,' said Annabelle. 'If the people knew that the plague doctor himself had succumbed, they would lose faith.' She indicated the adjoining room. 'Through here.'

Bill entered what she guessed was the medicine room. The walls were lined with shelves full of earthenware jars, bottles and thick, leather-bound books. The rest of the available space was taken up with desks and tables cluttered with medical instruments; oversized scissors, scalpels, pliers, clamps, forceps, spoons, hacksaws and dozens of devices which looked like the paraphernalia of a medieval torture chamber. On one of the shelves were a series of glass jars containing a misty fluid. Bill hurried over to give them a closer look, then realised they were being used to preserve bodily organs and bones.

'This is nice,' said Nardole, looking around like a child on a school trip. 'I like those.' He pointed to a row of skulls of what Bill guessed were dogs, cats and sheep.

'So you took your father's place?' said the Doctor.

'Four weeks ago,' said Annabelle. 'I have the learning, if that's your concern. He instructed me in all the teachings of Galen, the correct use of leeches and maggots. And I have all his books. So I continue his work, the best I can.'

'How's it going?' said the Doctor, idly picking up and sniffing a jar of herbs.

'I do all that can be done,' said Annabelle stiffly, as though she was trying to avoid revealing any emotion. 'But this plague, it defies understanding. In the past, after someone exhibited signs of illness, they would expire within four or five days. But this new scourge can overcome someone in a *matter of hours*, without any indication or reason. It has been endowed with a swiftness, a … perniciousness no mortal can resist. All my medicines and treatments have no effect.' Annabelle swallowed to regain her composure. 'I cannae save them. I cannot save a single soul.'

'You're worried about the people losing faith,' said the Doctor. 'But first you must have faith in yourself.'

Annabelle laughed bitterly. 'Sometimes I wonder if what I have been taught is even true. Maybe Mister Harvey's theories are right. Maybe disease is some contamination o' the blood, and not an imbalance of the humours.'

'Yeah,' said Bill. 'Maybe. Worth looking into, anyway.'

'No clues, Bill,' muttered the Doctor. He fixed Annabelle with eyes full of a thousand years of pain. 'You've lost your father. That's enough weight to carry on your shoulders. If there is nothing you can do against the plague, then there is nothing you can do. You're not doing anything wrong. You're not being found wanting. It's not your fault. Stop blaming yourself.'

Annabelle's expression softened, and for a moment Bill thought she might allow herself to cry. But then she turned away and busied herself tidying away some jars. 'The people are scared. Desperate. And I am the only hope they have left.'

'No,' said the Doctor. 'Reinforcements have arrived.'

Annabelle smiled ruefully. 'Is that why the King has sent you? He has heard of our plight?'

'There's something happening here, above and beyond the plague. Annabelle, what do you know about the ghosts?'

'I've seen them. I mean, everybody has. Anybody's who's lost somebody in the last month. The dead – those that have died of the plague – come back, to visit those they have left behind.'

'When exactly did it start?'

'It must be five weeks since the first ghost was sighted, in Mary King's Close.'

'Mary King's Close?' said Bill.

Annabelle nodded. 'That street was the first to be afflicted and has suffered the greatest. The ghosts return the night after the person has been taken away for burial on the Muir.'

'But without any news of the afterlife,' said the Doctor. 'Because they don't realise they're dead. They're just pale shadows of their former selves. What are they *for*?'

'I do not know,' said Annabelle. 'You should speak to a minister, not a physician.'

'Your father,' said Bill. 'Has he come back?'

'No,' said Annabelle. 'He is the only one I know of not to return. It's a pity. It would be a comfort to be able to talk to him, one last time. To ask his advice.'

'Yes, I'm sure it would,' said the Doctor. 'But there must be some other explanation. Your father, was he visited by the Night Doctor?'

'No.'

'I thought not,' said the Doctor. 'But you are aware of the Night Doctor, aren't you?'

'I have not seen him,' said Annabelle. 'But I understand that someone is … wandering the streets during the hours of darkness, calling on those with the plague, terrifying them half to death. People keep reckoning that it's me.'

'It's an understandable mistake,' said Bill. 'Since he's wearing your threads.'

Annabelle shook her head. 'Impossible. I keep the attire here, all the doors are locked and bolted and nobody enters or leaves during the night.'

'Maybe you share the same tailor,' said the Doctor. 'But the daughter of the couple we were with. Catherine Abney. Before she died, she was taken away by someone wearing your outfit. That wasn't you, by any chance?'

'No. I have never made any night calls. I have not stepped outwith this building after dark, because of the curfew …'

'Do you have any idea where the Night Doctor might've taken her?'

'One of the plague pits on the Borrowmuir, I suppose, or the Norloch. Does it matter?'

'It doesn't fit. And you know what I call things that don't fit? Clues.'

Suddenly the calm was interrupted by a series of urgent thuds coming from the hall. Bill was the first to make it out there, and realised someone was giving the door-knocker a serious seeing-to. 'Who is it?' she shouted back.

'The Doctor!' bellowed a man from outside. 'Where's the Doctor?'

Annabelle hurried out and unlocked and unbolted the door. She pulled it open, revealing one of the city guards, the same man who had arrested Bill the previous day. His chest was heaving. 'What is it?' said Annabelle. 'What's the matter?'

'The Lord Provost,' the man said, gathering his breath. 'Yer tae see him at once.' He then noticed the Doctor, Bill and Nardole standing in the hallway. 'Aw of ye!'

The Provost's house was a short walk away, located at the bottom of an alleyway near the Netherbow Port. The house had leaded windows with a lattice of panes and a thatched roof and looked more like a country cottage that had been shifted into the city than a townhouse. It even smelt of the countryside, thanks to the smoke of a bonfire in the nearby orchard.

The soldier knocked on the heavy iron door, and another soldier answered it and led them to the Provost's bedchamber. Annabelle went first; she had left her plague doctor outfit at home, explaining to Bill that the Provost knew of her father's death and she would draw less attention in her normal clothes. The Doctor followed her up the stairs, then Bill, and finally Nardole, who continued to exude the cheery air of a tourist.

Sir John Smith was a changed man. He lay propped against a pillow in his four-poster bed. His face was a deathly pale, his skin and hair were damp and his nightshirt was soaked with sweat. On his neck, Bill could see a cluster of dark blotches.

Even his voice was altered. 'Inside, inside,' he croaked, his voice thin. 'Doctor Rae, Doctor Stevenson. As you can see, all my endeavours have come to naught.' He gave a small laugh, which became a splutter and a cough.

The Doctor indicated for the soldier to wait outside, and once he had gone, the Doctor examined Smith, taking his pulse and temperature, and peering into his eyes.

'There is nothing that can be done for me,' said Smith weakly. 'The Lord has ordained this as my appointed time to be delivered from this state of sin. All I ask is that you make my passage to salvation painless and swift.'

'I'll see what I can do.'

Smith reached out to the Doctor. 'All I have done has been to try to save this town, to do the best for its people, you have to understand that . . .'

'I need you to be quiet.'

'Why?'

'I find self-pity deeply irritating.' The Doctor felt under Smith's armpit, then rolled back his sleeve to examine his arm, which was covered in bites. 'Yes. The usual cause of infection.'

'A surfeit of humours?' said Annabelle.

'If you like,' said the Doctor. 'You're the expert.'

'Then I must prepare a poultice to draw out the bile, and begin a blood-letting—'

'But, as you said, it wouldn't do any good.' The Doctor released Smith's arm. 'The onset, though, is quite remarkable. He shouldn't have got this bad this quickly.'

'Shouldn't I?' croaked Smith.

'As I said,' said Annabelle, 'this pestilence is possessed of a greater severity than anything before witnessed.'

The Doctor drew out his sonic screwdriver and levelled it at Smith's chest.

'What's that?' spluttered Smith.

'Just a fumigating torch of my own design. Don't worry, nothing occult-y.' The Doctor took a reading. 'No. It's bog-standard bubonic plague. No more lethal than normal.'

'That's … a great comfort,' groaned Smith.

The Doctor adjusted the screwdriver, then scanned Smith, starting at his head and working down to his stomach. 'Wait,' he breathed, and he adjusted the device again.

There was something on the man's stomach. What at first appeared to be a glistening blob of jelly, picked out in the sonic screwdriver's green glow. It was about a thirty centimetres in length, with serrated ridges and fronds at one end, gently waving as though it was underwater. With a shudder, Bill realised it was a living thing. The fronded end was a head and its mouth was attached directly to Smith's abdomen through a gap in his shirt. The rest of its body appeared to have been glued to the linen, rising and falling as Smith breathed in and out.

'What is it?' whispered Annabelle.

'Some sort of giant leech or lamprey,' said the Doctor quietly.

'I can see that,' said Annabelle impatiently. 'But what *is* it?'

'It's something not of this Earth.'

'You mean … it's from Hell?'

Smith looked down at the slug-like creature resting on his belly and groaned.

The Doctor gave Annabelle a pained look. 'I think that's a *little* unlikely.'

Now that she could see the leech, Bill could also hear it, a rhythmic squelching and gurgling as its oily body expanded and shrank. It was a parasite, and it was feeding on the Provost.

'What's it doing?' asked Bill. 'Drinking his blood?'

The Doctor shook his head. 'No, but it appears to have weakened his immune system. That explains the rapid progress of the infection.'

'Why can't we see it?' said Nardole. 'I mean, when we can't?'

The Doctor lifted the sonic screwdriver and the leech disappeared, leaving only the unappealing sight of Smith's pasty stomach and a patch of skin visible through the gap in his shirt. The skin was unmarked. There were no teeth marks or cuts. The Doctor ran his hand through the air where the creature had been and there appeared to be nothing there. He turned the screwdriver back towards Smith's stomach and the leech reappeared.

'Temporal displacement. It's there, but a microsecond out of phase,' said the Doctor. 'Must be a defence mechanism. Four-dimensional camouflage.'

'You mean, it's there but it's not there ... now ?' said Bill.

'That's a very good explanation,' said the Doctor. 'It's a gross simplification, but it'll have to do.'

'Can you rid him of it?' asked Annabelle.

The Doctor shrugged. 'What do you recommend? Salt? Fire? It's feeding on *something*, maybe if we could cut off the supply it would detach voluntarily, but what?'

'That's the thing that attacked you,' said Bill. 'Last night. Or one of them. I saw it.'

'Yes,' said the Doctor absentmindedly. 'I wonder ...' He lifted the sonic screwdriver away from the Provost and the leech faded away along with the sound of its persistent slurping. The Doctor straightened up and pointed the screwdriver at Bill's belly. It gave a low buzz, so he directed at Nardole's stomach, also to no effect. Finally, he aimed it at Annabelle's waist, and nothing appeared. 'You're all clear. Just making sure.'

'What about the Provost?' said Bill. 'He asked you here to treat him, what are you going to do?'

The Doctor nodded towards the Provost. Smith had fallen asleep with his mouth wide open. 'I think,' said the Doctor. 'We should leave him to sleep the sleep of the just.'

Chapter

8

Bill knocked on the door. While she waited for it to be answered, she glanced around the now-familiar close where she had first seen the ghosts. It looked ordinary in daylight; dingy, piled with rotting food, and with the occasional squeak and patter of a rat, but not remotely sinister. She was even getting used to the stink.

Bill heard someone clumping down the stairs, and the door opened. Betsy was not pleased to see her. 'Oh. It's yersel.'

'Sorry about running off last night,' said Bill, with her biggest grin. 'That's what I came to say. Sorry. About running off last night.'

'We were most concerned. Agnes in particular. There are things in this town at night ... ungodly things. A wee lass like yourself should take better care.'

'Yeah, tell me about it.' Betsy didn't reply, so Bill continued. 'Sorry. I mean that literally. Tell me about it. Can I come in?'

With a sigh, Betsy stepped back to allow Bill to enter. 'If you must. But you cannae stay long.'

'No problem,' said Bill, following Betsy up the stairs. 'I'm meeting a couple of friends later, we're doing a thing.'

'Aye, I suppose that's better than being alone.' They entered the main room where Betsy was prodding the fire with a poker, more out of habit than necessity. 'A'thing is better than being on yer own.'

'Yeah, fact,' said Bill nervously. Then, as casually as she could, she asked, 'Can I speak to Agnes? I probably owe her an apology too.'

'That'll no' be possible,' said Betsy. 'She's—'

'She's out,' said Bill. 'She's only here at night, isn't she?'

'What are you saying?'

'I thought so. I should've worked it out when she wasn't here last night. When you said she didn't like to leave the house.'

Betsy looked at her intensely. 'What Agnes likes or disnae like is none of your concern.'

'I'm sorry.' Bill could feel tears prickling in her eyes. Be strong, she reminded herself. Hold it together. 'When did she die?'

Betsy stared at her. 'She's no' deid.'

'You don't need to pretend any more, not for me. Please.'

Betsy busied herself preparing a meal, starting by chopping vegetables. 'Twelve days ago. She said she had a stomach ache, took herself off to bed. The next day, she had a fever, and the marks of the plague. After that, she grew weaker. I did my best to keep her warm, to make her comfortable. I held her, aw through that last night.' Betsy paused and gazed into the distance. 'She was so cold. Her breath was like … somebody dragging logs. And then … in the morn, she had been released frae her suffering. She looked so peaceful, like she was sleeping. Ten years younger. She was with the Lord.' She turned to Bill, her face crumpling in sudden grief. 'She's *gone*. My Agnes, she's gone.'

Bill rushed over to her and hugged her. 'I know. I know.'

Betsy returned the hug. 'It was sae fast. She knew what was coming, but she was so brave. For me. She was brave for me.'

'And then she came back? As a ghost?'

Betsy released Bill and nodded. 'The night after she was laid to rest. I was sitting here, alone wi' my thoughts, when I heard her calling. I looked outwith and there she was. Down in the close, looking up, asking to be let in.'

'So you did? Let her in?'

Betsy smiled at the memory. 'I could barely leave her outwith, could I? Aye, I let her in. She's my Agnes.'

'Her ghost.'

'Funny thing. She didnae ken she had died. But, passing away in her sleep, I suppose she wouldnae hae noticed …'

'You had a visit from the Night Doctor, didn't you? That night, before she died?'

Betsy nodded. 'They say awbody does.'

'Yeah.' Bill looked at her, at the kindly old woman with tears in her eyes. She couldn't tell her that the ghost Agnes wasn't the real Agnes. Maybe she already knew. 'So she comes back to you, every night?'

'She does,' said Betsy. 'Just after sunset. I leave the door open. Sometimes I fall asleep waiting, and she wakes me up. And then ... it's just like it was. Like nothing has changed. She sits there, in her old chair. And we gab through the night, about old times. She may seem a bit cold to you, but that's just her way. She never was one for the company, just the two of us. And when it's just the two of us ...' Betsy looked into the distance. 'Seeing her again, knowing that she's come back to see me, on her way to the Lord. I ken she's deid, and she'll leave me for ever one day, but being able just to say goodbye, it's a kindness.'

'She meant a great deal to you,' said Bill.

Betsy smiled at the memory, then changed the subject. 'You'd better be getting on to meet your pals. It'll be getting dark soon.'

'Yeah,' said Bill. 'Probably wise.'

'Where is it you're meeting them, if I may ask?'

'Street opposite the Old Tollbooth, near the Luckenbooths.'

'Which street?'

'Mary King's Close ...'

'You're no' to go in there,' said Betsy. 'Promise me, lass.'

'OK,' said Bill warily. 'Why? What do you know about it?'

'Only that it's the most corrupt and wanton street in aw of Edinburgh,' she said. 'Home to thieves, beggars, wastrels and harlots. The scum of the town. It's nae for nothing they call it the Street of Sorrows.'

'I'll bear that in mind,' said Bill with as much tact as she could muster.

'But that's no' aw they call it,' said Betsy, her voice rising in hysteria. 'Some say Mary King's is the very entrance t'Hell itself!'

The clock in the hall chimed ten times, then Nardole heard the creak of the stair behind him. He turned to see Annabelle descending carefully, lighting the way with a lamp.

'Are you still here?'

Nardole nodded and budged up the bench to offer Annabelle somewhere to sit. He'd been sitting in the hallway keeping watch ever since the Doctor had left at sunset. He hadn't even taken a bathroom break, something of which he was quietly proud. He briefly wondered whether he should, later on, tell the Doctor how diligent he had been, not taking a bathroom break, but thought better of it. It was enough that he knew. The satisfaction of a job well-done.

Annabelle remained standing, eyeing him with suspicion. 'What exactly are you doing?'

Nardole tapped his nose confidentially. 'The Doctor has a theory.'

'That's no' an answer to my question.'

Nardole heard a rustle of leather. He shushed Annabelle, took her lamp and extinguished it. The hall was plunged into almost total darkness, illuminated only by a pale beam of moonlight through the lattice window. The only shapes visible were the oak door and the plague doctor's cloak gently undulating as though disturbed by a draught.

'What is it?' whispered Annabelle, sitting silently beside him.

'The Doctor's theory,' said Nardole. 'Look!'

Slowly but surely, the left sleeve of the plague doctor's cloak began to rise, reaching up to the hook the cloak was hanging from. It lifted itself clear and floated backwards, hovering with the bottom a few centimetres above the floor. Then it reached up to one of the gloves, as though slipping an invisible hand inside it, and the glove twitched into life. The first gloved hand then fitted the second, and using both gloves the cloak reached up for the bird's skull mask. With one hand it held the mask in place, as with the other it drew up the cowl of the cloak, tucking it into the sides of the mask. Finally it reached for the wide-brimmed hat and placed it on top of where its head would be, securing the mask and the cowl with the chinstrap.

Nardole heard Annabelle give a gasp. In a panic, Nardole waved for her to remain silent, then froze, absolutely still, not daring even to change his facial expression.

The cloaked figure seemed to have registered the disturbance, as it slowly turned its masked face in their direction. It looked left and right as though searching with its empty, glass eyes, then began to slowly float towards them, its robe flowing on the wind. Nardole remained motionless, petrified, as the cloaked figure reached towards his face with a clawed glove ... then the claw continued over his head and collected the door key from the nail above him. The figure drifted over to the door and unlocked it with a simple, firm movement. The door opened with a gentle creak, no louder than the house settling in the night, and the figure floated out into the darkness.

'The Night Doctor,' said Annabelle. '*That*'s the Night Doctor!'

'And he's getting away,' said Nardole, fastening the toggles of his coat. 'Come on!'

Sir John Smith couldn't sleep. His head pounded and throbbed, his sores itched like they had tiny spiders inside them, and every movement elicited a spasm of pain. He was also finding it hard to breathe, his throat so dry and coarse, it felt as though he had swallowed a flagon of sand. Worst of all, there was the pain in his stomach, a gnawing sensation, like a knife being gradually twisted into a wound. That was where that creature was. Sometimes he imagined he could hear it suckling like a piglet, the sticky, saliva sound of it chewing at his guts. But when he looked down, when he felt the area, there was nothing there, even though he could feel its weight pressing down upon him.

So he sat up in bed, staring into the blackness. He had the plague. All his efforts to spare the town the pestilence had failed. All the measures he had taken had been in vain. All the men and women he had sent to be drowned and buried in the Muir had not been sufficient to keep the plague outside the gates. And all those deaths preyed on his mind. All the screams for mercy, all the tears, the fear in their eyes. Their faces kept returning to his thoughts, like ghosts of the mind. Ghosts of conscience. He reminded himself that he had no choice, that it was all for the greater good. That he was saving lives. But if that was the case, why was he so afflicted by the memories of those who had died? Why did he feel such guilt? And why had the Lord chosen to let him fall victim to the plague, when he was doing the Lord's work?

The answer was quite simple. He had failed the Lord. He had sinned, in thought and deed. He had acted out of pride. And soon he would be dead, one more body to be carted out of the Potterrow Port and dumped into a quarry-hole.

Smith was so absorbed in his thoughts, it took him several minutes to notice that he was not alone. A figure stood in the doorway of his bedchamber, its shape silhouetted by the illuminated hall beyond. He could make out a long robe, a wide hat, and a beak-shaped mask.

'Doctor Rae, is that you?' said Smith. His voice came out as a weedy croak. He drew in a deep breath to speak louder, but it hurt to raise his voice. 'Doctor Rae?'

The figure slowly shook its head from side to side.

'No, no,' said Smith. 'Guards! Guards!' His voice was little more than a gasp.

It was the Night Doctor. It had come for him. It entered the room, gliding without any discernible exertion. It didn't make a sound, moving without a footfall. It carried a long staff in one gloved hand, raised before it. Then it paused at the foot of his bed, barely visible in the darkness. It was watching him. Waiting.

'Ah, there you are,' said a familiar voice from nearby. A tinderbox flicked on, illuminating a man in a chair in the corner. It was Doctor Stevenson. He lit a lamp, filling the room with an orange glow, and sending hideous, giant shadows of the Night Doctor across the far wall.

'I've been expecting you,' said Doctor Stevenson cordially. 'How did you get in? Down the chimney or in through the backdoor? I'm sure a simple lock and bolt would pose no problem to a psychokinetic sock puppet such as yourself.'

The Night Doctor stared at the Doctor, the lamplight flickering in its eyes.

'Don't worry,' said Doctor Stevenson. 'I don't expect you to talk. Just pass on a message to whoever is pulling your strings. Tell them I'd like a word.'

The Night Doctor paused for a moment, as though considering the request, then drifted to the door as though caught in a strong gust of wind. Stevenson leapt to his feet and raced after it, chasing it out into the corridor, leaving Smith alone with his thoughts. Then, a moment later, Stevenson returned.

'All right!' The Doctor sighed and pressed a small pill into Smith's hand. 'Swallow this. And don't mention it to anyone.' Once Smith had swallowed, the Doctor hurried outside. Smith thought he heard him mutter 'Humans!' in exasperation as he left.

Chapter

9

Fortunately it was another clear night and the High Street was bathed in moonlight so Bill could make out the Old Tolbooth and the avenue of shops built into the side of it, the Luckenbooths. She looked back and forth up and down the street, hugging herself for warmth, the cold biting at her cheeks and turning her breath to clouds of frost. Then, at last, she spotted two figures running towards her, one of which had the distinctive shape and bouncy gait of Nardole, the other being Annabelle. She waved to them, and they joined her in the archway of one of the shops opposite the entrance to Mary King's Close.

'This is it?' said Nardole. 'Where you saw all the ghosts last night?'

'It was packed,' said Bill. 'They were queuing to get in, like it was the top nightclub.'

Nardole gave an 'oh well' shrug. 'Nothing on tonight, by the look of it.'

Bill peered out from under the archway to check the street. It was deserted. 'The ghosts were everywhere, there were hundreds of them …'

'Maybe we've missed them?' suggested Annabelle.

'No,' said Bill. 'I've been out here since sunset.' After leaving Betsy's house, Bill had returned to the High Street and watched as the Baileys of the Muir performed their grisly rounds, collecting more corpses for the plague-pits, making sure that she remained out of sight. Then, after they'd gone, a group of curfew guards had patrolled the street, luckily not bothering to check the archways too closely. But that was hours ago. Since then, she'd been completely alone with nothing but the Little Mix playlist on her phone to keep her amused. She had been expecting the ghosts to emerge from the side streets at any moment, but there was no sign of them.

'Maybe we're too early?' said Annabelle.

'No. If they were gonna be here, they'd have turned up by now …' Bill trailed off as she saw a figure running up the street. He had silvery hair and a long frock coat.

'Doctor!' called Bill. 'Over here!'

He hurried over to them. 'No luck with the ghosts?' he asked.

Bill shook her head.

'What about you, Nardole? Annabelle?'

'We saw the Night Doctor,' said Annabelle. 'Bill was right. He … it … is using my attire.'

'Called it!' said Bill.

'Then it vamoosed,' said Nardole. 'We lost it. What about you?'

'It turned up at the Provost's,' said the Doctor. 'Then I followed it here, but …' He paused, his eyes widening as he spotted something. 'Over there!'

Bill followed his gaze, towards the entrance of Mary King's Close. For a moment she didn't know what he had seen, then the Night Doctor slid from the shadows. It scanned the street, and Bill ducked behind a pillar. When she looked out again, it was in time to see the Night Doctor glide down the steps and disappear into the blackness of the alleyway.

'Well, if that's not acting suspiciously, I don't know what is,' said the Doctor.

He sprinted across the street with surprising speed. Bill pelted after him, the sound of Nardole and Annabelle's footsteps clattering behind her. When they arrived at the entrance to the alleyway, the Doctor pulled out a gas inspector's torch and switched it on. Bill switched her torch on too, and followed him down the steps. At the bottom, their torches lit up the narrow street winding away into darkness and the linen blankets draped overhead. It was just as it had been the previous night, even down to the feeling of there being some kind of force of pure malice, an impenetrable wall of blackness pushing her back. It was a combination of claustrophobia and the feeling of having one of your back teeth drilled, like hearing loudspeaker feedback inside your head.

Once again, Bill smelt something acrid and felt a blast of warm air. As they descended further down the street, she heard a young woman singing a lullaby to a crying child. It came from inside one of the houses, because the close itself was deserted. Bill sent her torchlight drifting up the walls of the buildings, up the wooden stairways and across the balconies, but there was no sign of life.

Then she saw the Night Doctor standing in the corner of the upper balcony. 'Doctor ...'

The Doctor had seen it. He gestured for them all to keep quiet and stay out of sight. Bill understood. If the Night Doctor was unaware of their presence, they should avoid drawing attention to themselves.

The Night Doctor raised its staff. Bill felt a prickling in her ear and, beside her, Annabelle also flinched.

The sound of crying grew louder as one of the upstairs doors opened. The young woman emerged and walked down the stairs. She had a wide-eyed, blank expression on her face and moved without watching where she was stepping, like a sleepwalker. Then one by one all the other doors in the close opened and their occupants emerged, all with glazed, blank eyes. They must have been summoned from their beds because they all wore nightgowns or the rags they slept in. They all slowly proceeded down the stairwells, in an orderly, seemingly choreographed fashion, those on the upper levels waiting their turn before joining their neighbours in the square.

Bill felt a finger tap on her shoulder and jerked awake. It was Nardole. She hadn't realised it, but she had been falling asleep too. Beside her, Annabelle also had a blank look on her face. Bill squeezed her hand, and Annabelle twitched and blinked as she woke from her reverie.

Then Bill felt a tide of sadness wash over her. It was as if she was suddenly remembering the loss of her mother all over again. Her mother's face. Her warmth. Her scent. The awful, aching absence. Bill looked up; she thought it had started raining. But there was no rain. Her cheeks were damp with tears.

She looked across at Annabelle. Tears streaked down both her cheeks, her face a grimace of pain. Then she heard a cry, a low moan. At first she thought it was an injured animal, like that time a fox got stuck in one of the canteen bins. But it was coming from one of the people in the square, the young woman holding a bundle of rags. She was sobbing so hard the muscles stood out in her neck. Her neighbours joined in, some sobbing, some howling. Even those not making a sound were weeping silently, the men's chests heaving, the women's eyes watering. They were all united in a pitiful, wretched chorus of misery.

Bill rubbed her eyes. 'I guess that's why they call it the Street of Sorrows.'

The Doctor shushed her, raised his sonic screwdriver and let it drift gently across the crowd. As he did, it revealed that each and every person in the square had something black and gelatinous curled against their stomachs. They each had a giant leech. As the Doctor switched off the screwdriver, the leeches faded away. 'All of them,' said the Doctor with a mixture of horror and wonder. 'It's a feeding ground!'

Then, like someone unplugging a stereo, the feeling of sadness fell away. It was almost too much. Bill found herself giggling with relief.

And everyone in the square laughed too. A single, uproarious laugh, in perfect unison. The men bellowed and the women shrieked, huge, gap-toothed smiles on all their faces. They fell about, choking with laughter, steadying themselves against the stairs.

Then as suddenly as it had begun, the laughter stopped. Dead. Everyone in the square froze, standing bolt upright, staring straight ahead, eyes wide open.

'What's happening?' said Bill.

'Not sure,' said the Doctor. 'It's inducing emotional responses, but why? An experiment? An evaluation?'

'Eh?'

'Or it's checking the settings. Like adjusting the levels on a telly to get the best picture ...'

Up on the balcony, the Night Doctor raised its staff. And Bill felt a rush of anger. How could this ... thing treat people this way? Use them as guinea pigs in some experiment? It was so wrong, so cruel. Just the injustice of it made her want to scream. To pull that staff out of the Night Doctor's hands and smash it. To kick him off that balcony.

The Doctor was looking at her with concern. He was almost as bad, bringing her here and then giving her a lecture on how they weren't to save anyone. What a hypocrite! How come it was all right for him to Time Lord it over people, but not her, because she was just a silly human, not like him. She could give him such a slap right now.

'Bill Potts,' said the Doctor gently. 'You're looking at me like you want to punch me in the face. Calm down.'

'I am calm,' said Bill, seething. She turned, to see Annabelle sneering at her like she was a piece of muck scraped off her shoe. 'And what are you looking at?'

'Ladies, ladies!' said the Doctor. 'Control yourselves.'

Bill swung her hand to slap him, but he grabbed it before it reached his cheek, and indicated for her to look at the people in the square. And then she saw. The people were all looking at their fellow residents with disgust and contempt. Their eyes were full of loathing, their teeth bared, sucking in mouthfuls of air in anticipation of a fight. Then a scuffle broke out between two men,

117

one shoving the other so he fell into the crowd, and suddenly the whole square erupted into a wild brawl, the men barging and wrestling, the women cursing and spitting.

Then one of the women pointed at Bill. 'It's her. The blackamoor! She's a witch! She's doing it, she's putting a curse upon us!'

How dare she disrespect her. Bill was ready for a scrap but the Doctor held her back. As he did, the people in the square abruptly broke off from their fighting to stare at her with unadulterated venom. 'Get her!' They clenched their fists and roared towards her.

'Run.'

The Doctor hauled Bill away, back up the street. Nardole and Annabelle were ahead of them, running through the winding corners of the alleyway. Bill glanced back – a crush had formed at the close entrance, as everyone tried to pile out at once. The Doctor pulled her hand and they kept running until they emerged into the sudden calm and silence of the High Street. Bill looked back, and to her relief there was no sign of anybody coming after them.

'Deep breaths,' said the Doctor. 'Count to ten.'

Bill counted to ten, and by the time she reached six, she felt like she was waking up, all the rage and hurt becoming a half-forgotten dream. 'Ten,' she said. 'What happened?'

Annabelle was also looking around curiously. 'The fury … What came over me?'

'Another induced emotional response,' said the Doctor. 'And a warning, to keep out.'

'It could've just asked nicely,' said Nardole. 'Or put up a sign. That would do.'

'Question is, what's down there that it doesn't want us to see?'

'Oh no,' said Bill. 'We can't go back, they'll kill us.'

'Unfortunately true,' said the Doctor reluctantly. 'We've done enough for now. We'll come back when it's light.'

'My kind of plan!' Nardole rubbed his hands and grinned. 'So, breakfast?'

There were four slow, heavy thuds on the door. At first Thomas thought he had dreamed the sound, remembering the time the Night Doctor had come for Catherine. He opened his eyes. He was in bed with Isobel, he could hear her breathing softly beside him. Then he felt it; the sensation in his stomach that had been there ever since they lost Catherine. The feeling of a great beast gnawing away at him, draining away all the hope, turning every day into a grey, joyless nothing.

There were four more heavy thuds on the door. So it was not a dream.

Isobel stirred in her sleep. 'Tam?'

Thomas grabbed his doublet from the chair and buttoned it over his nightshirt, then climbed delicately out of bed. If he wasn't wide awake before, he certainly was after his bare feet touched the cold floorboards. He collected the tinderbox and candle holder from beside the bed and lit a candle, shielding the flame to avoid disturbing Isobel. Then he pulled open the door to the main room and advanced into the darkness. The room was icy cold, the fire having died in the hearth.

There were four more thuds. Thomas padded over to the front door and opened it. And there was the Night Doctor, standing on the landing, just as it been the night that Catherine died. Just as it appeared to him in his dreams. It stared at him, giving no sign of its disposition or intent.

'What is it?' said Thomas. 'There's naebody sick here.'

By way of a reply, the Night Doctor stepped forward, forcing Thomas to back into the room. It lifted its staff, pointing it towards Thomas's stomach. As it did, he felt a stab of pain, as though something was biting him, followed by the heavy lead weight of grief.

'What's happening, Tam?' called Isobel from the bedroom doorway. 'What is it?'

'Get back to bed, Isobel,' said Thomas. 'This is no concern of yours.'

The Night Doctor shook its head and beckoned with its clawed glove for Isobel to come forward. She did so, in a reflex of terror. Then the Night Doctor raised its staff towards her head.

Isobel gave a sudden gasp, clutching her forehead as though lost, then with a sigh she lost consciousness and slumped. Thomas grabbed her by the waist to stop her falling. Then the Night Doctor aimed its staff towards his head.

'No,' said Thomas. 'Please. Whatever you're doing, I beg you, leave us be …'

The Night Doctor shook its head then stared directly at him with its empty, unseeing eyes. The point of the staff hovered barely two inches away from his face. Then Thomas felt like he was falling, toppling backwards into a deep well. Not sinking but rising, as though a great weight had been lifted from his shoulders. But what it was, he couldn't rightly remember –

Then the lamp fell from his hand and smashed, and there was nothing but darkness.

Chapter

10

Bill was woken by a hammering coming from downstairs. She pulled on her T-shirt and jeans and thudded down the stairs to the entrance hall. The Doctor, Nardole and Annabelle were already there and the bulldog-faced city guard was standing in the door. As she joined them, Bill noticed that Annabelle's plague doctor outfit wasn't hanging from the wall. She had half-expected to see it there and wondered where it had gone.

The soldier turned to leave with the Doctor, Nardole and Annabelle.

'What is it?' said Bill. 'What's happened?'

'The Lord Provost,' said Nardole confidentially. 'We've been summoned to see him at once.'

'Oh,' said Bill, grabbing her bomber jacket from the stool. 'So he's not dead yet, then?'

A short walk through the crisp morning air later, they arrived at the Provost's home. Their guard escort knocked on the door, and the guard inside let them in. Without a word, they made their way up the staircase to the Provost's chamber. As they reached the top, Bill exchanged a wary glance with Nardole. The Provost might not be dead, but what sort of state would he be in?

It turned out he was sitting up in bed in a fresh nightgown, a napkin tucked into his collar, a breakfast of eggs, pickled herring and thickly cut bread on his lap. He finished a spoonful as they entered, dabbing his mouth as he swallowed, indicating for the Doctor and Annabelle to come forward.

'Feeling better, I see?' said Annabelle.

Smith finished swallowing. 'More than that,' he declared heartily. 'As you can see, I have made a full recovery! I'm cured!'

'Quite extraordinary,' said Annabelle. She winced, as though suffering from a twinge of indigestion, then continued. 'I've never seen anything like it. For somebody to be so near to death …'

'And do you know what this means, Doctor Stevenson?' said Smith.

'No?' said the Doctor.

'It means I was wrong! It was not my appointed time. Quite the opposite. The Lord has, in his infinite grace, decreed that I am to continue in his service!'

'That's one explanation, I suppose.'

'There can be no other. All my efforts to deliver this town from the plague must be part of his eternal plan!' Smith chomped into a slice of bread with enormous self-satisfaction.

'Aren't you forgetting something?' said the Doctor.

'I don't think so ...'

'My little visit? Last night?'

'I recall the Night Doctor making a call,' said Smith. Then he peered at the Doctor with keen, devious eyes. 'But that's all ... Unless there's something you wish to add?'

The Doctor glanced around, noticing the two soldiers on guard by the door. 'No,' he said. 'There's nothing else.'

Bill stared at him. The Doctor must've saved Smith's life. And now he was trying to cover it up! 'But the Doctor, he gave you one of his magic pills ...'

'Oh, I think not,' said Smith disapprovingly. 'Because that would be witchcraft, would it not? And I would hate to have to burn Doctor Stevenson as a witch.'

'That's why you summoned us all here?' said the Doctor. 'So we could rejoice in your recovery?'

'I sent for you because I wanted you to realise that your ... censure of my activities was misplaced.'

The Doctor pulled out his sonic screwdriver. 'And that's it? No pangs of remorse? Nothing weighing on your conscience?'

'None at all,' said Smith. He scowled indignantly as the Doctor levelled the screwdriver at his stomach. Bill expected the slug-creature to reappear, but nothing happened. The Doctor adjusted the screwdriver, but still it failed to materialise.

'What is it?' said Bill.

'It's not there.' The Doctor frowned at Smith. 'You can't feel it?'

'No,' said Smith. 'Whatever it was, it has ceased its activities.'

The Doctor took a reading with the screwdriver. 'No, there's still a trace. Whatever it is, it's still here, somewhere in this room. With us.'

'What?' said Bill, looking around apprehensively, at the rough wallpaper, the piles of linen, the floral pattern on the ceiling, the washing bowl in the corner. She couldn't see anything, but then, of course, the creature was invisible. But she couldn't hear it either.

The Doctor circled on the spot, holding the sonic screwdriver at arm's length like a Geiger counter. 'It's close,' he muttered. 'Very close.'

'Doctor Stevenson,' said Smith. 'I would appreciate it if you left me in peace.'

The Doctor swirled dramatically, aiming the screwdriver at Smith's chest. Then he swung it back, towards Bill's stomach. She looked down fearfully, but thankfully nothing appeared. Then the Doctor waved it at Nardole's belly. Nardole gawped, but nothing appeared there either.

The Doctor shook his head and stalked around the bed. 'It's close. Very close. Seems to keep on moving …' Then suddenly he paused and pointed the screwdriver at his own stomach. And there, nestling against his waistcoat, was the black, slimy leech, the fronds on its head gently undulating, its body pulsating, bulges rippling along its length. Now that she could see it, Bill could hear it squelching and gurgling.

'Well, that's mildly unpleasant,' said the Doctor.

'Couldn't you feel it?' asked Bill.

The Doctor stared at her in disbelief. 'Yes, I could feel it, but I just thought I'd keep it as a big surprise. Bill, meet Mister Lamprey, my tummy buddy. *No of course I couldn't feel it!*'

'Sorry,' said Bill.

The Doctor switched off his screwdriver and the creature disappeared. Then he wafted his hand through the region where it had been, checking it had gone. 'That said … there is a mild sensation,' he said to himself. 'On the very edge of consciousness, a feeling you might disregard or attribute to being psychological …'

The Doctor trailed off. Then he twirled his screwdriver into a pocket and headed for the door, pausing only to call back. 'Thank you, Sir John Smith. It turns out this wasn't an entirely wasted visit. Oh, and you owe me a favour!' With that, he disappeared.

Bill turned to Nardole and Annabelle, who both looked as bewildered as she felt. 'Well, don't just stand there!' she said, and, pausing only to nick a slice of the Provost's freshly baked bread, she set off after the Doctor.

'You can't save anyone. Not even one man.'

'What?' said the Doctor, leading the way up the stairwell.

'Your lecture, remember? But you gave the Provost one of your pills too, didn't you? You cured him.'

The Doctor paused on the landing of the third floor. 'I did, yes. I know what you're going to say. Why save him? Because if anyone deserves to die, it's somebody like him, right?'

'No,' said Bill.

'Because that's not how it works. I don't decide who gets to live or die.'

'So why did you save him?'

'Because … because I could. Because if I'd let him die, that would've been my decision too. And nobody deserves to die, not even idiots.'

'Knew it,' said Bill. 'You can save as many people as you like.'

'No,' said the Doctor. 'He was the last one. That's where I draw the line.'

'If you say so.'

'I do say so. One or two we might be able to get away with, but no more.'

Bill shrugged and smiled. 'You're the Time Lord.'

'Yes, I am, Bill,' said the Doctor curtly. 'Thank you for reminding me.' He hurried up the next five flights of stairs, coming to a landing with a window that looked out over the city.

Bill leaned out for a better look while they waited for Nardole and Annabelle to catch them up. To the left, an imposing stone fortress rose over the rooftops. And to the right, the city sloped away, ending at the bottom of a huge, craggy outcrop, somewhere between a large hill and a mountain in size. Wisps of mist coiled over the cliff faces and overgrown scree slopes, while the summit was half-hidden in the cloud, a black ridge looming over the city.

The Doctor knocked on the door. 'It's me, the Doctor.'

Isobel opened the door. Seeing the Doctor, she smiled cordially. 'If you're calling about my Tam, he's feeling better.' Seeing Annabelle, she added. 'After his ... food poisoning.'

'I'm glad to hear it,' said the Doctor. 'But that isn't my reason for calling.'

'No?' Isobel stepped aside to welcome them into her home. 'Then what is it?'

The Doctor ducked under the door and Bill followed him inside. Thomas was sitting by the fire, repairing a boot.

'Something else I wanted to check,' said the Doctor. 'Would you mind standing up?'

Thomas placed the boot on the floor and stood up. 'Doctor, there's nothing wrong wi' me, even the buboes have cleared up …'

'And let's halt our little journey to Too Much Information-Ville right there. Can you hold still for me for a moment?'

Thomas straightened up, his arms by his sides, and the Doctor directed his sonic screwdriver at the man's midriff. Another of the leeches appeared, fastened to Thomas's stomach. But this leech was tiny and shrivelled, its fronds parched and brittle, like dry leaves.

'Oh my Lord,' said Thomas, staring down at the apparition. 'What's that?'

'You have a parasite. Don't worry, it's not necessarily a sign of poor hygiene. Nardole, the tongs.'

Nardole fetched the tongs from the fireplace as the Doctor adjusted the mid-section of his screwdriver. 'If I can de-interlace the phase displacement …'

'Devil talk!' muttered Thomas.

'Technobabble,' snorted the Doctor. The screwdriver produced a high-pitched wail. 'Now, Nardole.' Nardole reached out with the tongs and gingerly clasped the leech in its pincers. It fell away from Thomas's stomach, revealing a circular maw ringed with rows of serrated teeth. Nardole then took a step back, holding the leech at arm's length, not sure what to do with it.

'Put it in the corner,' the Doctor told him, and Nardole gingerly placed it on the floor. Then the Doctor turned to Isobel. 'Now you.'

Isobel looked at him fearfully. 'Naw ...'

'Don't worry, it won't hurt. It didn't hurt, did it, Thomas? Just a little de-lousing.' He raised the screwdriver, and another leech appeared on her stomach. Like the other, this one was also scrawny and brittle. The Doctor made the sonic screwdriver squeal, and Nardole darted forward to remove the creature with the tongs, placing it beside the other in the corner.

'What are thon things?' said Thomas.

'I'm not entirely sure,' said the Doctor. 'But what's interesting is that they seem to be inert and atrophied. As though their source of nourishment has been cut off ...'

'Their source ... was us?' said Isobel, regarding the two shrivelled masses with disgust.

'*Was* being the crucial word. Past tense. They were feeding on you. But now something's changed. What?' The Doctor peered at Isobel. 'Do you look different?'

Isobel blinked in surprise. 'No ...'

Bill gave Isobel a proper look. She did look different. Her eyes were clear and sparkling and there was colour in her cheeks. She looked like she'd had a decent night's sleep for the first time in weeks. And Thomas too. 'They look … happy.'

'Aye,' said Isobel. 'My man's just been saved from the plague, by the mercy o' the Lord!'

'Because … your daughter …' said Annabelle.

'Daughter?' said Thomas.

Isobel shook her head, not understanding.

'Your daughter, Catherine,' said Annabelle. 'She died nine days ago. Of the plague.'

Isobel laughed incredulously. 'We dinnae hae a daughter. Ye dinnae ken what you're talking about!'

'Aye, I think we'd remember,' said Thomas.

'Yes,' said the Doctor gravely. 'I think so too. I think that's what's changed.'

'But you must remember her,' said Bill. 'She came back to you as a ghost.'

'A ghost?' said Thomas. 'Of a daughter we never had?'

A chill ran down Bill's spine. Thomas and Isobel weren't pretending or confused. They genuinely had no memory of their daughter. Her entire existence had been taken away from them. 'Doctor. It's like she's been … deleted from their heads.'

'Hence the bonhomie.' The Doctor turned to address Isobel. 'You had a house call from the Night Doctor last night, didn't you? Oh, don't bother, your memory of the visit was probably deleted too.'

'I mind I was visited, when I was sick, but ...' Thomas trailed off as the Doctor placed his fingers on his forehead and peered deep into his eyes. 'Oi, what ...'

The Doctor frowned in concentration, closing his eyes. 'No. No, not a memory wipe. She's still there, under the surface. It's just your access to the memory that's been blocked. You don't know she exists, so you can't remember her.' He opened his eyes. 'You're lucky. Whoever did this took a short cut. It's reversible.'

'We dinnae hae a daughter!' said Thomas defiantly. 'I'd remember!'

The Doctor had a jolt of realisation. 'Yes! Yes, of course! That's what it was doing last night!'

'Which was?' said Annabelle.

'It was trying to make the population work through the stages of grief. Depression. Anger.' The Doctor turned back to Thomas. 'And ... denial. Remove the source of the grief and all is sunshine once more!'

'You mean, the Night Doctor is ... trying to cheer people up?' said Bill.

'Or stop them being unhappy. Not quite the same thing,' said the Doctor.

'But why?'

'Maybe it's just being nice,' suggested Nardole.

'Well I hardly think *that's* likely,' said the Doctor. 'How long have you been travelling with me?'

Nardole pulled a face and wandered over to look out of the window.

'The leeches!' said Bill. 'Maybe it's cheering them up to get rid of the leeches!'

'Well done,' said the Doctor. 'Now you're thinking empirically. Thomas and Isobel forget their daughter, suddenly their parasites no longer have a source of nourishment. Conclusion?'

'The creatures were feeding on their unhappiness?'

'Grief-leeches!' declared the Doctor. 'Literally. Leeches of grief. They feed on misery! Futility and despair with a side order of angst.'

Annabelle crossed the room and crouched down to examine the two dead leeches, her nose wrinkling. 'So these creatures take away the grief? They cure it, like drawing out an excess of a humour?'

'An excess of melancholy?' The Doctor considered the idea, and nodded. 'If you like. But, no, they don't cure it, any more than a leech cures you of having too much blood.' He crouched down beside Annabelle and tapped one of the creatures with his index finger. It rolled over stiffly. 'But do they prevent their hosts from feeling anything else, from feeling anything *other* than grief? Maybe they block out any positive emotions, any hope, any joy, any peace of mind? Because they want the misery to remain on tap! An endless supply, they don't want it to run out! They want their hosts to remain grief-stricken for as long as possible, on the very brink of despair. Not too little, not too much.'

'And they're responsible for the rapid onset of the plague?' asked Annabelle.

The Doctor considered. 'By accident rather than design. Lack of REM sleep, depressed white blood cell count ... The host's body can't fight off infection, it gets an easy ride.' He grinned as another idea popped into his head. 'And, of course, this city would be the ideal feeding ground. So many people losing loved ones, parents, brothers, sisters, sons, daughters. Rich pickings. That's why the Provost was rejected.'

'Cos he was too smug?' said Bill.

'The parasite was only drawn to him because of all his guilt and self-pity. Once that was gone … it had to seek out a new source of nourishment. The strongest source of grief in the vicinity.'

'You?' said Bill.

The Doctor gave a sad smile. 'I've been around a bit, you know. You don't live for as long as I have without losing some friends along the way. Without accumulating a few regrets.'

'And one or two broken hearts,' said Nardole tactfully.

'One or two,' said the Doctor wistfully. 'I am slightly over my baggage allowance, shall we say? Which makes me the top dish on the menu. The house special!'

'Is that's why they're here?' asked Bill. 'Cos it was like a big buffet?' The Doctor stared at her like she had just said that unicorns exist. '... of death?'

'They're not native to this planet. Ergo, they were brought here, or landed here by mistake, or they've always been here. One of the threeeee!' Suddenly he doubled up in pain and directed his sonic screwdriver at his waist. The leech that appeared was fat and glistening with saliva, its fronds undulating like the tentacles of a sea anemone. 'There's only one way to find out!'

'Actually, there's probably loads of ways,' said Bill.

'Take this,' said the Doctor, tossing the screwdriver to Bill. 'Keep it on the creature, it has to remain in phase.'

Bill nodded and held the screwdriver steady. She glanced at the others. They were all staring at the Doctor, wondering what he would do next.

The Doctor braced himself against the wall, then reached down and grasped the leech by its head, the creature's skin squelching like he was gripping wet mud. His fingers sank into its flesh, its fronds wrapping themselves around his wrists. The Doctor grimaced, baring his teeth, and made a snarling noise. 'Oh, my wee, sneaky, cowerin' timorous beastie. What ... are you?'

The creature continued to writhe under his fingers, slick with glue. The Doctor craned his head back, his eyelids fluttering. 'Yes! That's you! Intelligence!' he cried triumphantly. 'You've got a mind! That's good, something to talk to. Questions, please! Give me questions!'

Bill was momentarily lost for words, her only thought to wonder why the Doctor hadn't told her what to ask in advance. 'Um … what do you want?'

'To feed,' groaned the Doctor. 'Isn't that obvious, I'm a parasite! Next question!'

'Where are you from?' said Nardole.

'Don't know. It was hot. And dark!' groaned the Doctor. 'Something more specific, please!'

'How did you get into the town?' asked Annabelle.

'We crawled,' said the Doctor with a growl of agony. 'We scented grief. So much sorrow! A feast of despair!' He shook his head from side to side. 'It's fighting me. Last one!'

'Mary King's Close,' said Bill. 'Was it Mary King's Close?'

Instead of a reply, the Doctor gritted his teeth. 'Now, Nardole!'

Nardole gawped at him blankly. 'What?'

'Get it off me! The tongs!'

Nardole took a deep breath and grasped the leech in the tongs. The creature fell away from the Doctor, and Nardole stood holding it, not sure what to do. Then the leech hissed at him and Nardole recoiled in shock. He proceeded to stumble about the room, knocking into the chairs, mumbling in panic. 'What do I do? What do I do? Aaargh! It's looking at me! I don't like it!'

'The window!' shouted the Doctor.

Nardole backed over to the window, poked the creature through it, and with a tentative cry of 'Gardy-loo!' opened the tongs. The leech fell out of sight. Nardole watched it drop, then turned towards them with the grin of someone expecting a spontaneous round of applause. 'Well, that went well!'

The Doctor steadied himself and looked at Bill. '"*Did it come from Mary King's Close?*" It's a grief-leech from outer space! It can't read *street signs!*'

'I didn't know that,' said Bill. 'How was I supposed to know that?'

'But you may be right,' admitted the Doctor. 'I got the sense of … a concentration of grief so overwhelming it led to a feeding frenzy. The Street of Sorrows seems as good a candidate as any.'

'But how did it get there?' said Annabelle.

'It came from somewhere hot and dark,' considered the Doctor. 'Narrows it down.'

'You got rid of it,' said Bill. 'You made it release you. How?'

'Obvious, isn't it?' said Nardole. 'He cut off its food supply by thinking happy thoughts.'

'Quite the opposite,' said the Doctor. 'It found it had bitten off more than it could chew. I gave it too much darkness, it got indigestion. Let's go.'

'No,' said Thomas, stepping into the Doctor's way. 'There's something you hae to do first.'

'There is?'

'You said we had a daughter.' Thomas looked at his wife, who reached out her hand. He took it. 'And our memories of her hae been blocked? Can you gie them back?'

'I can,' said the Doctor. 'But are you both sure that's what you want?'

'How could we no' want to mind our daughter?' said Isobel.

'Because,' said the Doctor. 'You may never be happy again. You will have to live with that sadness for ever. It's your choice.'

'We already ken we had a daughter,' said Isobel. 'You told us. So the only choice is for us to spend the rest of our lives kenning we had a daughter and forgot about her, or remembering her. And I couldnae live with no' kenning.'

'Nor me,' said Thomas. 'We hae a right to ken. And her life … we hae to mind her, or it'll be like she never lived at all.'

'Very well,' said the Doctor. He took a deep breath and stepped forward, spreading the fingers of his left hand on Thomas's forehead. He furrowed his brow, then released Thomas with a small shove before repeating the process with Isobel. Then he stepped back to evaluate his work.

Thomas turned to his wife, his eyes pooling with tears. She looked at him, smiling in agony. 'Catherine.' She buried her face in her husband's chest, and he rocked her, staring into the distance, shaking his head as though trying to rid himself of the pain.

Bill brushed a tear from her eye. The cruelty of making them go through the grief of losing their daughter all over again. But there was no other way. She looked to the Doctor, and indicated that they should leave without a word.

'Ermmm!' exclaimed Nardole in alarm. As he spoke, Bill heard a slithering, slurping sound coming from the corner of the room. The two leeches were not dead. They were standing on end and swaying from side to side as they scented the air, their tube-like mouths revealing rows of hook-like teeth. They streaked across the floor like rats, heading for Thomas and Isobel.

'Their grief. It's woken them up!' said Bill.

In a flash, Annabelle snatched the tongs from Nardole and grabbed one of the leeches in its pincers. She lifted it into the air, where it shrieked and hissed in protest, and flung it, hard, into the fireplace, where it landed with a crunch of wood and a sputter of sparks. Without a moment's hesitation she lunged and grabbed the second leech, hurling it into the fire to join its sibling. The two creatures melted away like overcooked soufflés, shrivelling to a blackened crisp.

For a moment, nobody said anything. Then Annabelle returned the tongs to their place by the fire. 'I have a duty of care,' she said. 'Those things are a health hazard.'

Bill found it hard to disagree. Nardole edged towards the door, and Bill opened it to go. But before they stepped outside, Thomas released his wife, and placed a hand on the Doctor's shoulder. The Doctor regarded him with incomprehension.

'Thank you, Doctor,' said Thomas. Beside him Isobel smiled sadly, and added. 'Thank you for giving us our daughter back.'

Chapter

11

Mary King's Close was no more appealing in daylight. A short shower had turned the gutters to mud and water dripped from the linen blankets still hanging across the alleyway. As they descended, Bill looked upwards at the windows that were just holes; the bulging, crumbling daub; and the clumps of mould on the underside of the extensions, all propped up by rotting brackets. The walls were caked in soot deposited by countless lamps and streaked with years of dribbling rainwater. Occasionally Bill could hear the squeak and scamper of rats as they hurried into their hiding places beneath the decaying piles of vegetable peel and smashed jugs.

The air was stagnant but surprisingly warm, and as they got nearer to the close, the acrid smell of rotten eggs grew stronger, until Bill felt like it was burning the back of her throat. But this time, in the grim half-light of day, she could also see a faint, mustard-yellow gas drifting up into the sky.

The Doctor sniffed. 'Sulphur dioxide. Someone either has a very experimental approach to baking or ...'

'Or?' said Bill.

'Or we've located the source of this street's infernal malediction.'

'Eh?'

'He means it's bad for your health,' said Nardole helpfully, gawping at the teetering houses. 'Bit quiet. Where is everyone?'

'Here, the plague has been uniquely potent,' explained Annabelle. 'Every household has been touched to some degree. Some claim it is retribution for the sins of those who live here.'

'"The most corrupt and wanton street in all of Edinburgh",' said Bill, recalling Betsy's warning.

'But they're wrong,' said Annabelle. 'The plague shows no discretion between the virtuous and the wicked. It comes for everybody, from the highest to the low. The difference is, down here, the people are already bedevilled with other infirmities of the flesh, they are already suffering from malnutrition, so they are more vulnerable to the infection, and once infected, the plague's progression is a' the swifter.'

'Sounds like you're on to something,' said Bill. 'Environment and diet, isn't it?'

'Bill,' said the Doctor. 'No clues!'

'Sorry. Forgot the Time Lord code.'

'But Annabelle *is* correct.' The Doctor circled on his heels, raising his voice as though he was back in the lecture hall. 'The squalor would make this neighbourhood uniquely predisposed to the plague and the resultant suffering. Hence the abundance of grief-leeches. We're standing in the unhappiest street in town!'

'So where is everyone, when they're at home?' asked Nardole again.

'At home,' shrugged the Doctor. 'Confined to barracks.'

'Too afeart to step beyond their doors,' said Annabelle. 'Those that remain are in fear for their lives.'

'Ghosts of the recently departed turning up every night can't help,' said Bill.

'Here!' said the Doctor, ushering them towards one of the buildings. 'The really terrible smell! It's coming from over here!'

Bill and the others joined him outside a low doorway. The Doctor was right; the rotten egg smell was overpowering. She held a hand over her mouth, until Nardole helpfully handed her a handkerchief.

The Doctor buzzed the sonic screwdriver at the door, but it had no effect. 'Doesn't work on wood!' the Doctor muttered. 'Right. Brute force it is! Nardole, if you could do the honours?'

Nardole looked around in surprise, doing a 'Did you mean me? Really?' mime. Then he grinned and sauntered nonchalantly to the door. He considered it for a moment, weighing it up like an expert, even making a viewfinder with his fingers, then he casually booted his foot through the bottom of the frame. The door fractured, and it only took another two kicks to shatter the rest.

'There you go,' said Nardole casually. 'Tarovian kickboxing. It's a hobby.'

The Doctor stooped to enter the building, and even Bill had to duck to get through the low doorway. Inside, it took her eyes a few seconds to adjust to the dark. Her first impression was that the floor was unusually smooth, consisting of flagstones covered in fine sand or dust. There were pillars every few metres and numerous barrels and troughs full of grain. At one end there was a semi-circular alcove in the stone wall, which Bill guessed was an oven, meaning it was an abandoned bakery.

Nardole coughed to get Bill's attention, and she turned to see the Doctor disappearing down some steps into the cellar, interrogating the darkness with his electric torch. She switched on her own torch and followed him down the steps.

The cellar was cramped and cluttered with rubbish: split barrels, smashed jugs and torn sacks. At one end there was a hole in the ground, about a metre in diameter. The sides of the hole were rough and uneven, suggesting that the floor had crumbled away. There was a constant draught of hot air blowing out, like the vent of an underground boiler.

The Doctor directed his torch at the hole but it failed to penetrate the blackness.

'Hot and dark,' he said, his torch illuminating his opening-a-Christmas-present grin. 'I think we've found where our little friends came from.'

Yeah, thought Bill. And I think we've found out why they call it the entrance to Hell.

The hole led down into a cramped tunnel. It was barely wide enough for Bill to squeeze through, so she had no idea how Nardole managed it, but she could hear him puffing and groaning behind her, his duffel coat scuffling against the rock walls. Annabelle was the next in line behind Bill, while the Doctor led the way, the beam of his torch fluttering in the darkness.

After a few minutes, the tunnel grew wider, and Bill became aware of a sucking, slithering sound, like somebody wading through Swarfega. When the tunnel opened into a cave the size of a small coffee shop, her worst fears were confirmed. It was crawling with grief-leeches, hundreds of them, heaped against the walls, squirming and sliding over each other, their fronds writhing like seaweed. As her torchlight picked them out, they hissed at her, opening their serrated mouths wide. There was another tunnel on the far side of the cave, but the leeches covered every centimetre of the ground. To get through, they would have to walk through them.

'I've got an amazing idea!' said Nardole as he caught up with them.

'Go on,' said the Doctor quietly.

'We turn back. Leave in the TARDIS. Put it all down to experience.'

'OK,' said the Doctor. 'Let's stick a pin in that for now. Any other ideas?'

Bill spotted some round objects beneath the wriggling mass. 'Look. Eggs.'

'Yes,' said the Doctor. 'I think we've found their nursery.'

'I've got it,' said Bill. 'It's obvious, isn't it? Duh! We just walk through them, thinking happy thoughts.'

'Happy thoughts may be a big ask,' said Nardole. 'What with the whole …' He indicated the seething mass of glutinous leeches in their path.

'Yes,' said Annabelle. 'It's hard enough just to go on, with all that I've seen. All the good people I've lost. I do not think I could put it out of mind.'

'That may not be necessary.' The Doctor prodded one of the leeches with the tip of his shoe. It hissed at him then slithered aside.

'They're not interested in us?' said Bill.

'They're not hungry,' said the Doctor. 'They've already fed.'

'Mary King's Close?'

The Doctor nodded. 'They're satiated. Sleeping off a heavy lunch. That's why we can see them. They only go out of phase when hunting or feeding.' The Doctor took another step, and another, until he was ankle-deep in the sluggish leeches and had to nudge them out of the way in order to move.

'You're sure happy thoughts won't make any difference?' said Bill. 'Cos, you know, I might just do that anyway.' Then, pressing her lips together and wincing, she took her first step into the oily, wriggling mass. She was careful not to let her torchlight rest on any of the creatures for too long, for fear of waking them up, but just enough to avoid squashing one underfoot.

'Waa-ooh! Eeeuch!' moaned Nardole from behind her, suggesting that he had begun to make his way through the leeches too.

Bill paused and turned back to give Annabelle an encouraging smile. 'It's all right once you're in.'

Annabelle took a deep, uncertain breath, and stepped forward. Fortunately for her, the Doctor, Bill and Nardole had partially cleared a path, revealing some of the rocky floor, so she didn't have to push any of the leeches out of her way.

While Bill ... the area in front of her was thick with the leeches. At least a thirty centimetres deep. So she did the only thing she could. She lifted her right foot, and then gently lowered it into the mass, nudging the creatures aside with the tip of her shoe, letting her foot sink deeper and deeper into the clammy, wriggling mass, letting it rise up around her ankles until it covered the bottom half of her leg.

Ahead of her, the Doctor reached the tunnel and some higher ground. He held out his hand and after two more agonising steps into the leeches, Bill grabbed his hand, and he pulled her onto the solid ground beside him.

Bill looked back, still making sure not to let her torchlight linger or to shine it in Nardole or Annabelle's faces. Nardole was grimacing, making 'Eeeuch!' noises like a holidaymaker who has stepped into some seaweed while paddling in the sea. His tongue was out and his teeth bared, a picture of utter panic. Then he came within arm's reach, and Bill helped the Doctor pull him to safety.

Nardole took a deep breath and grinned. Then his face fell. 'Oh no.'

'What is it?' asked Bill.

'I've just realised. This is going to be the only way out as well, isn't it?'

'Oh, probably,' said the Doctor.

Annabelle had reached the middle of the cave, and to her horror, Bill saw one of the leeches clinging to the woman's exposed leg. Annabelle patted it away and it fell into the mass of other leeches. Then she walked forward stiffly as the leeches began to lift their necks to hiss and spit at the intrusion.

'So they might not be satiated on the way back,' muttered Nardole.

'Nearly there,' said Bill, offering a hand to Annabelle.

Annabelle brushed it aside and made the last step unassisted. As she joined them, Bill thought she even saw her smile. 'Right, that's done,' said Annabelle. 'Let's be getting on, shall we?'

Chapter

12

Nardole considered humming to lighten the mood, but thought better of it. The Doctor had warned him about humming before. In fact, he had even thrown Nardole out of the TARDIS into deep space and left him drifting in a spacesuit for five minutes to make the point. But the silence – apart from the scuffle of their footsteps and the occasional *plip!* of water – felt almost as oppressive as the foul, fumy air. Of course, Nardole's lungs could filter out the sulphur dioxide content; he felt no discomfort. He just didn't like the pong.

The Doctor and Bill were leading the way, followed by Annabelle, with Nardole keeping up the rear. He kept wondering whether he should ask Bill to lend him her torch, because he could barely see where he was going, and kept tripping over bumps and banging his head on the tunnel roof. But he was not one to complain. Because that was another thing he had been thrown out of the TARDIS for. That, and winning at table tennis.

'Interesting,' said the Doctor, and their little party halted as he shone his torch over the tunnel wall. He caressed the rock thoughtfully with his fingers. 'This tunnel is a natural phenomenon.'

'So?' said Bill.

'This is a lava tube. Formed by molten rock, flowing from an eruption.'

'What eruption?'

'How far have we walked, would you say, Bill? About a mile?'

Bill shrugged.

'Due east,' said the Doctor. 'Which puts us …'

'Directly under Arthur's Seat!' said Annabelle.

'Arthur's Seat?' said Bill.

'You must've seen it, big mountain at the end of the High Street,' said the Doctor. 'Named after … well, someone called Arthur.'

'And it's a volcano?' exclaimed Bill.

The Doctor rubbed a finger on the wall and tasted it. 'Carboniferous. Last eruption … two hundred million years ago, give or take.'

'You mean it's extinct,' said Bill. 'Dormant.'

'So are a lot of things,' said the Doctor darkly. 'Before they wake up.'

Annabelle looked fearful, so Nardole took her aside. 'Don't worry about him. He likes to be all doomy, so he can look clever if things go wrong.'

Annabelle nodded. 'A pessimist.'

'A pessimist who frequently looks clever,' said the Doctor. He knelt down and prodded the remains of a leech shell. 'The leeches came this way. We are, without wishing to be egregiously literal, getting warmer.'

Suddenly a deafening howl came from somewhere in the darkness ahead of them. It was like the entire brass section of an orchestra playing different notes at once. Then it came again; a deep, echoing, stomach-shaking roar.

The Doctor spun around, pointing his torch into the darkness ahead. Bill did the same. Nardole and Annabelle huddled behind them. And then, with a stampede of heavy feet that shook the ground, the creature emerged from the darkness, only halting when it was fixed in the torchlight. It was a huge, fur-covered elephant with enormous curved tusks. It stood about three metres tall, as high as the roof, blocking the width of the tunnel. It lifted its trunk and snorted, and Nardole felt a blast of moist air on his cheeks. He could even smell it; it reeked of stale dung.

'A mammoth,' said Bill. 'What's a woolly mammoth doing down here?'

The mammoth snorted and bellowed. Nardole covered his ears until it had stopped.

The Doctor lifted his sonic screwdriver and buzzed. 'It's not doing anything.'

'What?' said Bill.

'It's another ghost. Another psychic projection.'

'A ghost?' said Annabelle, pausing as the mammoth gave another deafening roar. 'But it's ... there! I can feel its breath!'

'And smell it,' added Nardole. 'Whiff. Oh dear!'

'Your senses are being hacked,' said the Doctor. 'Your brains are being told that you can feel it and smell it and they're so stupid they'll believe anything.'

'Again, rude,' said Nardole.

The Doctor stepped forward like a matador inviting the mammoth to charge. 'Well? Come on, then?' The mammoth exhaled heavily, ruffling the Doctor's hair, but the Doctor didn't seem to notice. 'No,' he said. 'You'll have to do better than that.' He reached out to pat the mammoth's trunk – but his hand passed straight through it, as the creature was no longer there.

Bill swung her torch around the cave. It was empty, there weren't even any marks on the floor. 'So we all imagined it?'

The Doctor shrugged. 'A hologram, a group hallucination, split the difference. The point is, it was *induced*.'

'You mean it was made by someone?' said Nardole.

'Precisely,' said the Doctor.

'Or some ... thing,' added Nardole ominously.

'... or something, yes, thank you. Always good to keep our options open.' When he thought Nardole wasn't looking, the Doctor pulled a face and waggled a finger at the side of his head.

'I saw that!' said Nardole.

'Why would someone – or something – conjure up a beast like that?' asked Annabelle.

'A deterrent,' said the Doctor. 'Go away, keep running, and don't, whatever you do, come back.'

'Which means there's something down here?' said Bill, looking into the darkness.

'Oh yes,' said the Doctor. 'Something that doesn't want to be disturbed. I wonder what?'

Nardole had a few ideas but decided to keep them to himself. The Doctor would rather he asked another question. 'So it chose a mammoth because …?'

'Probably the most frightening animal it could think of, indigenous to this area …'

'It's not indigenous,' said Annabelle. 'I've never seen one before.'

'Well, no, you wouldn't. They died out ten thousand years ago.' The Doctor peered into the gloom. 'Probably designed to deter the first settlers. Somebody needs to update their firewall settings.'

'Firewall?' said Bill. 'This isn't going to be the only thing it throws at us?'

'Oh, I very much doubt it,' said the Doctor. He put away his sonic screwdriver and stalked down the tunnel. 'We should stick close together and keep on our toes.' He turned back, grinning wildly. 'This is going to be fun!'

After a few more minutes, the tunnel narrowed even further. Bill let Nardole and Annabelle go ahead, partly so she could keep an eye on them but mainly so that she could keep checking there wasn't anything coming up behind her. She didn't want to mention it to the Doctor, he'd think she was being silly, but she kept getting the feeling there was something following them. Something a few steps behind her. But whenever she looked back to see what it was, her torch just illuminated an empty tunnel, disappearing into blackness.

The fact that the air still stank didn't help. Her throat was burning and she was desperate for a glass of water. Or just an electric fan, that would help. But they'd –

Bill stopped. She felt it again. A presence behind her. A couple of centimetres away from her spine, between her shoulder blades. She turned, half-expecting to see a leech or another monster, but there was nothing there. Just empty tunnel. Sighing with relief, she turned back – to find that the Doctor, Nardole and Annabelle had disappeared.

They must've left her behind. 'Doctor?' Bill called. 'Nardole?' There was no reply so she hurried forward, letting her torchlight dance over the rock walls to make sure she wouldn't miss any side tunnels. But within a few metres the tunnel narrowed to no more than half a metre wide. Bill peered into the gap. 'Doctor? Hello?'

There was still no reply. Bill glanced back at the empty tunnel. Weirdly, it seemed to be narrower than she remembered. Bill retraced her steps, and after a couple of metres, her torch lit up a rock wall blocking the tunnel. Bill ran her fingers over it. It was solid, cold stone. But there couldn't have been a rock fall, she would've heard.

Bill guessed she must've got disorientated. Going forward, there was only the half-metre-wide gap, so that must be how she had got in, so it must be the only way out. She peered into the passage, checking it was clear, then squeezed in. The sharp rocks on either side pinched into her waist. But after a few metres, the tunnel narrowed even further, to no more than a 30 centimetres wide. Bill turned sideways and shuffled into the gap, but then her jacket caught on something. She twisted back, to pull it free, but rather than her torch lighting up the tunnel she had come down, it showed another rock wall, no more than a 30 centimetres away from her.

Bill reached out and touched it. Solid, cold stone. She wriggled her jacket free, then decided to try going further into the gap. But after a few more centimetres, it became so narrow that she got caught again. She shifted and jostled her elbows to turn the torch so it would light the way ahead. It lit up another rock wall.

There was a rock wall ahead of her and another behind her? This section of tunnel she was in was only 30 centimetres wide – no, less than that, both sides of the cave were pressing against her – and only about a metre in length. If she reached out, she could touch the wall in front of her and the wall behind her. And they were both solid, cold stone.

Looking up, there was more jagged grey rock. Bill shuffled to try to get free, but somehow she got herself stuck even tighter with the wall pressing against her chest. She tried to return to her previous position, but just felt the wall on the other side pressing into her back.

She looked around. Ahead, 30 centimetres away, solid rock. Behind, solid rock. She was stuck in a passage barely wider than her body. Completely alone.

Bill tried to remain calm. The only sound was her own breathing. Shallow, hoarse, becoming more and more rapid.

Then she dropped her torch and everything went dark. She tried to bend down to reach it, but the rock walls were too tight around her, she could barely bend her knees. And the walls were tight against her elbows, pressing her arms into her sides. The more she struggled, the less room there was to move. She turned her head, and felt the rock wall against her nose, and when she tried to turn back, her head was jammed in position. Jammed tight, flattened against a solid rock wall.

'Doctor,' said Bill. 'Doctor. I can't …' She pushed and strained all she could, but to no avail. 'I can't move. I can't move!'

Then she felt a bony hand on her shoulder. It pinched her hard and pulled her backwards, and she found herself slipping onto the tunnel floor.

A torch flashed in her face, forcing her to close her eyes. When she opened them again, she was looking into the concerned faces of Nardole, Annabelle and the Doctor.

The Doctor held out a hand and hoisted her to her feet. 'Are you all right?'

'Yeah, awesome,' said Bill. Nardole bent down and retrieved her torch from the floor and handed it to her. 'I just … Where did you all go?'

'Where did we go?' said Annabelle. 'Where did you go?'

'You fell behind,' explained Nardole. 'So we came back for you.'

'No, I was stuck, trapped in a …' The more Bill tried to explain it, the less sense it made. 'The walls were closing in.'

'Yes,' said the Doctor. 'Claustrophobia. Another psychic firewall. But you're through. The tunnel widens out in a bit. Ready to move?'

'You just watch me,' said Bill. She shone her torch ahead of her, and the tunnel did indeed widen out. She set off down it, determined. 'This time I lead the way.'

* * *

Annabelle watched the dark girl disappear into the darkness, then, as the Doctor moved, she followed. Not for the first time she asked herself what she was doing, going along with this strange Doctor and his two students. If that's even what they were. The Doctor did not comport himself like a medical professional, while the notion of a young girl being openly permitted to study medicine struck her as unlikely, even disregarding the young girl's colour. She didn't even dress like a gentlewoman; having removed her leather jacket, she was now wearing nothing more than trousers made of sackcloth and an indecently tight shirt marked with the word BAZINGA, whatever that meant.

As for the third one, Nardole, he was the strangest of all. He appeared to have no hair at all, not even any eyebrows, and even in the heat of the tunnel remained clad in a giant buttoned wool-coat. He seemed to treat everything with a cheerful stoicism, as if exploring underground tunnels and coming face to face with ancient beasts was all in a day's work.

And what was she doing down here, with them? What did she hope to find? She couldn't help feeling that her time would be better spent caring for her patients, those afflicted by the plague. But then she remembered that there was nothing she could do for them, except try in vain to relieve their suffering, and she felt the familiar gnaw of guilt at all those she had seen die. It was easy for the Doctor to say it wasn't her fault, but she knew – her father's books told her – that those with the plague *could* be cured, so why had all her efforts failed? And yet the Provost had recovered without her intervention, when every indication was that he would die. She had a strong feeling the Doctor and his friends knew more than they were letting on. And that, she realised, why was she had gone with them. To find out what they weren't telling her.

Ahead of her, Bill had stopped. As she approached, Annabelle saw the reason why. A yard or so ahead, the tunnel sloped steeply downwards, then dropped away completely to become a vertical shaft with walls of sheer rock. The Doctor and Bill's strange lights made no impression on the darkness, but Annabelle had the strong sense that the well, if that's what it was, must be hundreds of feet deep. Even looking at it, she felt her body swaying out of her control. She gripped the tunnel wall to steady herself.

'Well, that's it,' Bill said. 'We'll have to turn back.'

'The leeches came this way. They couldn't have climbed up a sheer cliff. Conjecture. They didn't.' The Doctor edged forward, his boots scuffling on the inclined ground. He dug in his pocket and retrieved an apple, then threw it forward into the shaft. The apple vanished into the blackness and, if it hit the ground, it did so without making a sound.

'If we had a rope ladder we could descend, but without would be suicide,' said Annabelle. 'There's not enough handholds, and I'll gladly admit, I'm not one for heights.'

The Doctor backed away from the edge, much to Annabelle's relief. 'Of course not. Feeling a bit dizzy? Queasy sensation in your stomach, legs starting to wobble? Trying to resist the urge to jump?'

'Something like that,' said Annabelle.

'Thought so,' said the Doctor. 'The wild beast. Claustrophobia. Vertigo. We're working our way through the primal fears.'

'So what do we do?' said Bill. 'Climb down?'

The Doctor exhaled dismissively. 'Down where? All we have to do is make a leap of faith.'

'Oh, right. Like in *Raiders of the Lost Ark*.'

'What?'

'There's this bit in a cave, where there's this chasm and – oh no, wait, it's the other one, the one with Sean Connery, oh God, what's it called?'

'Let me know when this gets relevant. My attention is drifting.'

'But Indiana Jones makes a leap of faith and it turns out there was a stone bridge there all along, except he couldn't see it, because it was painted to look like it was the opposite cliff.'

The Doctor stared at Bill as though she was mad. 'And, presumably, at that point everyone in the cinema shouted out, "But that would never work! Because of depth perception!"'

'No. And remind me never to take you to the cinema.'

'I'm not sure I'd want to, if Indiana Jones is indicative of your quality threshold. Oh, wait! Does he only have one working eye?'

Nardole ahem-ed. 'So what *are* we going to do?'

'We go on,' said the Doctor matter-of-factly.

'What?' said Annabelle.

'We close our eyes, take a little run, and jump.'

'But we'll fall,' Annabelle leaned forward to gaze down the bottomless shaft. 'You saw the apple.'

The Doctor took a short run-up. 'One, two, three!'

Annabelle stared in horror as the Doctor jumped over the edge and plunged into the blackness. Then she held her breath, waiting for the sound of his scream or the thud of him hitting the ground. But there was nothing.

'I'm fine, thanks for asking!' The Doctor's voice called out of the darkness. 'Well, come on!'

Bill gave a final look at Nardole and Annabelle, then jumped into the void. Again, there was no sound of her landing. Instead, there was the crunch of an apple. 'It's OK,' said Bill.

Nardole closed his eyes, and walked forward. Annabelle watched as he disappeared into the darkness. Then a delighted whoop echoed up the shaft.

So, thought Annabelle. A leap of faith is required. Time to show she still had some faith in herself. She felt sick to her stomach but closed her eyes and took a tentative step forward. The ground dropped away beneath her, and she felt herself toppling forward. She wanted to open her eyes, to pull herself back. But instead when she lowered her foot it came to rest on solid ground.

She opened her eyes to find she was standing a little way further down the tunnel with the Doctor, Bill and Nardole. Looking around, she realised that the tunnel *was* the shaft. Somehow, something had made it appear vertical, when it was more or less horizontal.

'All right?' the Doctor asked. Annabelle nodded. 'Good. It's not easy to overcome hard-wired instincts. Requires willpower and a developed frontal lobe.' He waved his torch along the tunnel, and shouted out, 'Any more, or is that it? How about some logic puzzles? Maybe a maze? Or hopscotch? Hopscotch is always good!' The only reply was the echo of his voice.

The Doctor prepared to move on, then suddenly stopped. 'Wait.' He switched off his torch and indicated for Bill to follow suit. She turned off her light, and Annabelle expected to be plunged into darkness, but instead she could still see the Doctor, Bill and Nardole, all illuminated by an orange glow coming from somewhere up ahead.

'This is it,' said the Doctor gravely, advancing towards the light source. 'I think we've reached our destination . . .'

Chapter

13

The tunnel led to a cavern the size of a university lecture hall filled with pools of swirling, bubbling lava. Every few seconds, one of the pools spurted, hurling molten rock several metres into the air. The rock then splattered down into the burning sludge where it was churned and folded under the surface layer in readiness for another burst.

The lava pools filled the chamber with a pulsating orange glow, giving it the appearance of being inside of a living creature. And in the centre was the creature's heart, a squashed sphere caked in cooled lava, with a dozen twisting arteries extending outwards and into the cavern walls like the flying buttresses of a gothic cathedral. They too were coated in a black, tar-like substance, but with the lowest extremities draped in what looked like wrinkled blankets but which Bill realised was solidified lava. The squashed sphere appeared to have once had a sea-urchin-like form but lava had congealed over most its spines, leaving only a few needles visible.

Bill paused at the edge of the chamber. She wasn't sure whether to continue, as the ground between the lava pools consisted of just a smooth crust of solidified lava which might or might not hold her weight. She turned. Annabelle was taking in the chamber in dumbstruck awe, while Nardole had the indifferent look of a sightseer who would rather be reading the guidebook. The Doctor, of course, was smirking like this what exactly he had been expecting all along.

Bill nudged him. 'It's a spaceship, isn't it?'

'Possibly. Whatever it is, it's been here quite a while,' said the Doctor.

'You recognise it?'

'No. New one on me.' The Doctor pointed to the underside of the squashed sphere, which was encrusted in the fragments of shells, like smashed barnacles. 'But look. That's how the leeches got here.'

'They hitched a ride?'

'I think that's very unlikely,' said the Doctor. 'No thumbs.'

'You know what I meant. Piggybacking.'

'I think it crashed,' stated Nardole, pointing.

Bill tried to see what he was pointing at and, in a break in the mist, she saw there was a fracture down the side of the sphere, which weirdly made her think of a Christmas pudding with a slice taken out. It was hard to see, but inside there appeared to be a nest of coiled roots and branches.

'Let's find out, shall we?' The Doctor made his way towards the spaceship, jumping nimbly along one of the struts from the ship that extended at ground level. The lava had cooled over it and formed a ridge.

If it could take his weight, it could take hers. Bill carefully began to make her way across, using her arms to balance. And trying not to look at the slopping, burning pools of volcanic porridge on either side. One slip and she would be toast.

She reached the spaceship, and climbed inside. What she had taken for roots and branches were the innards of the ship: its capillaries and its nerves, twisted and tangled. It was like standing inside a hawthorn bush. While they waited for Nardole and Annabelle to join them, Bill tentatively touched one of the branches. Under the slightest pressure, it cracked and crumbled away. Bill recoiled with a guilty gasp.

'The ship,' she said. 'It was a living thing!'

'Let's not jump to conclusions,' said the Doctor. 'It still might be.'

'Messy, isn't it?' said Nardole, as he heaved himself in. He blew some soot off one of the desiccated branches. 'Someone should go over this place with a dust-buster. What? Just saying.'

'What is it?' said Annabelle. 'I've read of … strange formations in caves, but nothing like this.'

'Ah. But this is not of this Earth,' said the Doctor. 'This fell from the stars.' There was a way through into the interior of the spaceship, and the Doctor led the way, carefully parting the branches.

'The heavens, do you mean?' said Annabelle.

'Haven't you read *The Man in the Moon* by Francis Godwin?' said the Doctor. 'It must've been published by now? In hardback at least?'

Annabelle shook her head.

'Spoiler. Chap travels to the moon in an engine carried by swans. Well, this is like that. But without the swans.' The Doctor paused. 'You should read it. It's a real page-turner. There's a great bit where he travels to the moon in an engine carried by swans.'

'I'll make a note of it,' said Annabelle quietly as they emerged into the central chamber of the spaceship. It was a circular chamber with a high arched roof and a floor sloping into the middle. In the centre was what appeared to be a giant natural sponge, about a metre high. It gently pulsed with amber light and was honeycombed with holes, as though it was made of pumice stone. It was certainly brittle, as chunks of it had broken away and lay crumbled on the floor. And, just as the spaceship had had branches extending out of it into the cave wall, the sponge had numerous branches extending into the walls of the chamber. The walls were also a giant amber honeycomb and reminded Bill of a photo she'd once seen of the inside of a bone. It was, she thought, like standing inside an enormous Crunchie bar.

The sponge had no obvious controls, but it was clearly the nerve centre of the ship because all the branches were leading off from it. The Doctor had to part them in order to make his way into the centre of the chamber and allow Bill and the others to join him.

'So what do we do now?' said Bill, crouching down to examine the giant sponge. 'Is there an on switch? A log in?'

'We say hello,' said the Doctor. He called out. 'Anyone home? Shop!'

'What is happening?' said Nardole plaintively.

'Not now, Nardole,' said the Doctor.

'Why are you here?' said Nardole.

'Not now,' said the Doctor impatiently. 'I'm trying to make contact with an alien life form.'

'An alien life form?' said Nardole.

'Yes, the big round thing we're standing inside. Have you not been paying attention, I'm not sure how I can make it any clearer.'

'You're standing inside me,' said Nardole.

Suddenly the penny dropped. The Doctor's eyes widened. 'Ah!'

'It's speaking through Nardole,' said Bill. 'It's using him to communicate!'

'Of the four of you, his psyche is the least troubled,' said Nardole. 'And he was happy to oblige.'

'Well, that's Nardole for you,' said the Doctor. 'Selfless to a fault. Is he unharmed?'

'Oh yes,' said Nardole, regaining his normal chummy disposition. 'It's quite nice, actually. Sort of tingly. Like having a bath in warm lemonade …'

'So who am I addressing?'

Nardole went back into a trance. 'I do not know. If I had a name, it has been lost to me.' He turned to them each in turn. 'Do you have names?'

'Yes. People call me the Doctor. This is Bill Potts.'

'Hello,' said Bill, not sure whether to address Nardole, the big sponge in the middle of the chamber or the chamber in general. 'Wotcha!'

'And this is Annabelle Rae,' said the Doctor, indicating Annabelle. 'Nardole, you've already met.'

'And why are you here?' said Nardole flatly, as though half-asleep.

'To help, of course,' said the Doctor. 'If help is needed.'

'And find out about the ghost thing,' said Bill. 'And the Night Doctor, what's that all about?'

'Because of the relentless pain,' said Nardole.

'Relentless pain?' said the Doctor, concerned.

'Their pain. The humans. It is too great to bear,' said Nardole. 'It is … poison.'

'Poison?'

'Their pain becomes my pain. Their suffering, my suffering. But it is too much to endure!'

'Empathy!' exclaimed the Doctor. 'Of course. You're attuned to the ambient psychic field. Powerful emotions create the greatest psychic disturbance and there are no emotions more powerful than grief. And you're receiving it all, aren't you? Full volume, all channels! You're in direct empathy!'

'I share their pain,' said Nardole. 'All their regret, their fear, their … heartache.'

'And it's overwhelming, isn't it? Like they're all screaming at once … and you can't shut it out. You can't switch it off, can you?'

'I cannot close my mind to the suffering of others, even if I wished to.'

'Yes!' said the Doctor. 'I know what you are. A Psycholops!'

'A what-o-lops?' said Bill.

'Psycholops. A space-bound race, they migrate between the stars in immense shoals, bound together in a psychic gestalt. That's how they communicate with each other, they sense and share their emotions. Bit like the Isolus, if you've ever heard of them.'

'I haven't,' said Bill, looking around, marvelling at the honeycomb ceiling. 'So this isn't a spaceship, then? This is all part of the … Psycholops?'

The Doctor nodded. 'They may have been sentient spaceships once. Maybe they were genetically engineered and evolved to become a species. It's funny how life takes over. But no, not a spaceship now.'

'Yes,' said Nardole. 'I am Psycholops. Once I had a thousand sistren. Now I am alone.'

'I'm very sorry to hear that,' said the Doctor. 'So what happened to you? How did you end up down here?'

'I acquired an infection,' said Nardole. 'It weakened my will, separated me from my family, and in my diseased state, I drifted into the gravitational field of this world. And I fell.'

'Like you said,' said Annabelle. 'It came from the heavens.'

'Bringing the leeches with it,' said Bill. 'The infection!'

The Doctor prowled around the chamber, addressing the ceiling. 'And, let me guess, when you landed the planet was in a grip of an ice age. The only locals were primitive hominids hitting each other with sharp rocks. So you set up a psychic barrier to keep them away.'

'I did not wish my infection to spread,' said Nardole. 'So I buried myself away and entered hibernation, sustaining myself with the heat of the mantle plume beneath the surface. And while I remained dormant, so did my infection.'

'That was very public-spirited of you,' said the Doctor. 'That's empathy for you. So then you napped for, what, ten thousand years? Fifty thousand? Meanwhile the glaciers retreated, any trace of your existence was obliterated, and those primitive hominids evolved higher cognitive functions, invented the haggis and built a city on top of you. Am I right?'

Nardole nodded.

Bill smiled to see the Doctor now entering 'lecture mode'.

'But then something disturbed your sleep. The plague. Oh, but not just any plague, the worst plague Edinburgh has ever seen. Not a single household is spared. People are cut down without rhyme or reason. The old, the young, the righteous and the wicked. People believe that their God is either testing them or he has turned his back. There is no hope, no redemption, only remorse and the fear of not knowing who might be next in line. A vast upwelling of grief. Without precedent, without respite, without end.' He paused. 'Right again, aren't I?'

Nardole nodded. 'I was reawakened six weeks ago. And as I ceased to be dormant, so did my infection.'

'And, scenting lunch, the leeches burrowed their way out to Mary King's Close.' The Doctor halted, troubled. 'But what about the ghosts?'

'I think I've got it,' said Bill. It was her turn to address the ceiling. 'You're trying to reduce the level of grief cos it's poisoning you, right? So what do you do? You try to take away the source of the grief – which is that people have lost their loved ones – by *bringing them back as ghosts!*'

Nardole nodded.

'With Betsy and Agnes, and Thomas and Isobel and Catherine ... The ghosts are supposed to be a comfort, aren't they? To solve the problem of too much grief! Not to make people happy, just to make the problem go away!'

'Death, where is thy sting-a-ling-a-ling?' remarked the Doctor.

'And the Night Doctor?' said Annabelle.

The Doctor whirled. 'Animated by the Psycholops here, in order to visit those who are about to die and scan in their brains and bodies, so it can make a perfect recreation. Well, almost perfect. As they're scanned before they die, they don't remember that bit; they think they're still alive.' He rounded on Nardole once more. 'But it hasn't been working, has it? Ghosts turning up unexpectedly on people's doorsteps, not quite having the desired effect?'

Nardole sadly nodded. 'I don't understand it. It works for some, but for most, it only makes the grief worse.'

'Well, of course, what d'you expect?' said the Doctor, his accent becoming thicker as he became more indignant. 'How is anyone supposed to come to terms with losing someone if they're being *haunted* by them! Do you know what you're doing? You're exacerbating their suffering. Tormenting them. Twisting the knife. Taking those dearest to them and bringing them back as a ... supernatural tribute act! An ersatz *parody*? What's the matter? Weren't they upset enough, you had to go and turn it up an extra notch? Weren't things *spooky* enough for you?'

'I only wanted to end the suffering.'

'Yeah. You only did what any unfeeling idiot would do,' muttered the Doctor. 'All that empathy and you don't understand a thing.'

Bill still had questions to be answered. 'So that's what you were doing in Mary King's Close. Why you made Thomas and Isobel forget their daughter. You're trying to find another solution?'

Nardole nodded. 'And I have done. If I take away the memories of everyone in the city, I can take away their grief.'

'No,' said the Doctor. 'Not happening, I'm afraid. Off the table.'

'Why not just save them?' said Annabelle indignantly. 'Why not just cure the plague?'

Nardole looked tearful. 'I don't know how. I don't understand the processes of death.'

Bill exchanged a look with the Doctor. What? 'You don't know about death?'

Nardole shook his head sadly. 'It is not something I have any experience of. Nobody wants to die. Those who left behind suffer as much, if not more. So why do people have to die?'

'Because …' The Doctor paused. 'I could give you a list of reasons. Philosophical, religious, biological. Take your pick. But it's just the way it is. And it is, quite frankly, deeply annoying.' He softened. 'But sometimes it's a mercy, too. An end to pain.'

'I cannot endure it,' said Nardole plaintively. 'I can feel it eating away at me. Corroding me. Poisoning me. I think that I am going to die.'

'I'm sorry,' said the Doctor. 'I wish I could help you.'

'Can't you just, I don't know, fly away?' said Bill.

Nardole shook his head. 'I cannot leave.'

'Doctor, what about if we TARDIS him out of here?' whispered Bill.

'Well, should I ever be able to overcome my objection to the word "TARDIS" being used as an active verb, I suppose it might be possible ...'

'You don't understand,' said Nardole. 'I cannot leave. I *must* not. While I was dormant, the pressure of the plume beneath me increased. It continues to grow and it requires all my spare energy to hold it at bay. If I were to leave, or cease to be alive ...'

'All that pressure would be released,' said the Doctor bleakly. 'In a big, catastrophic explosion.'

'You mean you're sitting on the volcano, stopping it from going off?' said Bill.

'I am acting as a plug on the main vent, yes. I am using my psychokinetic power to maintain the physical integrity of this geological feature.'

'And the fact that you're being poisoned by all the grief means you're getting weaker?'

Nardole nodded sadly. 'I estimate the eruption will destroy everything in a radius of twenty miles.'

'Everybody in Edinburgh would perish,' said Annabelle breathlessly. 'It would be the tragedy to end all tragedies.'

'The anguish would be overwhelming,' said Nardole. 'I cannot allow that to happen.'

'Forget what I said earlier,' said the Doctor. 'You're not a monster. You're a hero. The little boy saving the town by sticking his finger in the dyke. All this, you've done out of kindness.'

Nardole looked up at the ceiling. 'So you see, I have to wipe their memories. I don't want to do it. But I must, if it's the only way of saving them.'

'And would it work?' said Annabelle curiously.

Nardole smiled at her appreciatively. 'It worked for Thomas and Isobel Abney.'

'People can't mourn what they don't know they ever had,' said the Doctor. 'But – and this is the important thing – given the choice, they would rather have the grief. They would rather spend the rest of their lives in mourning than lose a single memory of those they have lost. Because there is nothing more precious than those memories. They are all that they have left of their loved ones. And it is with those memories that they keep them *alive*.'

'I told you, I don't understand the processes of death,' said Nardole glumly.

'You can't do it,' said the Doctor. 'You don't have the right. You can't take people's memories away from them. And if you try, I won't let you.'

'But if I don't, their grief will poison me,' said Nardole. 'And I will not be able to contain the volcano and they will all die.'

The Doctor bit his thumb in frustration. 'There has to be another way. Leave it with me.' He grinned secretively. 'Well, I said I'd help you, didn't I?'

Bill noticed that Annabelle was staring in fascination at the central sponge. Then, as though in a trance, Annabelle reached out to touch it.

'I wouldn't do that, if I were you,' Bill warned her, but she was too late. Annabelle sank her hands inside the sponge and gasped in pain.

Suddenly the ground trembled and the chamber light dimmed almost to darkness before pulsing with greater urgency.

'Doctor ...' said Bill.

'No,' moaned Nardole, as though in great pain. 'No, no, make it stop ...'

The Doctor darted around to stand behind Annabelle. 'She's plugged herself into the Psycholops' central nervous system. Annabelle? Annabelle!' She did not reply, but remained still, her back rigid, her breathing shallow. 'All right, brute force,' said the Doctor. He grabbed her wrists and started to pull.

'No,' said Annabelle. 'If I am detached from the brain-core, I will die.'

'What?'

Annabelle turned to face the Doctor and said, quite calmly, 'If I am detached, I will die. You will kill me. I will die.'

'Annabelle, something tells me you're not quite yourself,' said the Doctor. He dug out his screwdriver and buzzed it at her. It revealed a large, distended jet-black leech hanging from her stomach, its length snaking up around her back, up her spine and between her shoulder blades, with its head resting on Annabelle's head. Its mouth was firmly attached to the top of her skull. Its fronds twisted in her hair.

'She had one of the leeches all along!' said Bill.

'No,' said the Doctor, releasing Annabelle's wrists. 'I checked her when we first saw the Provost, remember. She must've acquired it somewhere along the way.'

Annabelle smiled. 'You were right, Doctor. The creature that was attached to the Provost sought out a new source of nourishment. You were already providing succour for another of my kind, so it chose the next strongest source of grief. The town doctor.'

'Ah, yes,' said the Doctor. 'The person who has seen the most death and suffering. The person who carries the weight of the whole town on her shoulders. The person who people look to for hope … when she has no hope in herself.'

'Wait,' said Bill. 'You're saying the Doctor already had a leech at that point? Sorry to be all "fridge logic" here, but where did it come from … Oh, hang on. It was the one that attacked him in the street, right?'

'Yes,' said the Doctor. 'Ever since then, I've been walking around, blissfully ignorant of the fact that I was host to a parasite. Well, perhaps "blissfully" is the wrong word. But that's how it works, isn't it? The host has to remain oblivious. They have to go on thinking that the reason they never stop being miserable is because there is something wrong with *them*.'

'And that's why all those leeches in that tunnel let us just walk straight through them,' said Bill. 'They *wanted* us to come here!'

Annabelle smiled. 'And you didn't suspect a thing.'

'So now I have the honour of talking to a grief-leech by proxy,' said the Doctor. 'So much easier than a mind-link. You're accessing Annabelle's speech centres, I take it?'

Annabelle's smile remained fixed to her face. 'I have penetrated her frontal lobe with my radula. I have access to all her thoughts, emotions and memories. They are … delicious.'

'It's eating her brain?' said Bill, horrified.

'It's a brain parasite,' said the Doctor. 'What do you expect?'

Nardole doubled up, clutching his head with a howl of pain. 'No! Stop it! No!'

The Doctor turned back to Annabelle and snapped 'What are you doing?'

'I am not devouring this woman's sorrows. That would be *indulgent*. No. I am stimulating her brain to increase them.'

'What?' The Doctor was horrified. 'You're *amplifying* her grief? But why?'

Nardole gasped. 'Doctor … she is injecting it, directly into me, into my mind!'

'Saturating your psyche!' He turned back to Annabelle with a vengeful expression. 'But if you kill the Psycholops, it won't be able to hold back the eruption. It'll destroy the city!'

Annabelle smiled. 'Yes. I know.'

'Which will wipe out you and all your grief-leech buddies. I don't mean to be a harsh critic but it strikes me that you haven't thought this through.'

'Some of us will survive,' stated Annabelle. 'When the people flee in terror, they will take us with them. And then we will escape into the world.' She smiled at the thought.

'Why haven't you done that already?' said Bill. 'Oh. Cos of the quarantine. Nobody enters or leaves. I'm just answering my own questions here, aren't I?'

Annabelle turned to face her. Bill noticed that the woman's face was growing paler, her eyes reddening, her cheeks becoming even more sunken. 'Yes. We have been confined to this city. But when it is destroyed, the neighbouring towns and villages will be consumed with grief. We shall find new hosts, and feed, and reproduce. We will spread across this miserable planet. And its misery shall be ours for the feasting!'

'All very unpleasant I'm sure,' said the Doctor. 'As if the human race don't have enough to worry about without a bunch of invisible parasites noshing away on their sadness.'

'We know enough to know there is a bountiful and endless supply,' said Annabelle. 'Their history is a parade of cruelty and privation. Even now, the land is consumed in a war, setting brothers against brothers, fathers against sons.'

'Which you seek to exploit.'

'Then at least it would gain a purpose,' said Annabelle with a cruel smile. 'Our nourishment!'

'Spoiler. The civil war won't last for ever.'

'There will be other wars,' said Annabelle. 'Other famines, other plagues, other disasters, natural and unnatural.'

'And if they stop being unhappy, what then? You incite another war? You send one of their rulers mad?'

'I hardly think that will be necessary,' laughed Annabelle. 'There will always be death and destruction.

It is part of human nature. We need do nothing but take hosts. Humanity's own greed and insularity will take care of the rest. They are the architects of their own misery. We are simply putting ourselves at the top of the food chain.'

'Taking advantage of the suffering of others. It's obscene.'

'It is a fundamental law of nature,' said Annabelle. 'Everything is food for something. We cannot be condemned for acting according to our genetic imperative. We have evolved to be the way we are. We have no choice, we must feed or die. Whereas humans have a choice and they choose to cause suffering to their own kind. That is the *obscenity*.'

'You have a seriously messed-up view of humanity,' said Bill.

'It is not my opinion,' said Annabelle coldly. 'It is the opinion of Annabelle Rae.'

'You're just saying that.'

Annabelle raised her eyebrows. 'Believe what you wish. It makes no difference. The human race will be our new hosts!' She arched back and closed her eyes in exultation, as though entering a trance.

Nardole cried out. 'No. Doctor. Stop her.' The ground began to shake and the chamber was plunged into darkness.

The Doctor came to a decision. As the light returned, he turned off the sonic and the leech disappeared. Then he grabbed Annabelle by her elbows.

'Doctor, you can't. That thing said it would kill her,' said Bill.

'It might be bluffing,' said the Doctor. 'If it kills her, where's it going find a new source of food?'

'You?'

'Even if it was telling the truth, we don't have any choice,' said the Doctor urgently. 'If the Psycholops dies, disaster.' He began to tug at Annabelle's elbows.

She opened her eyes and smiled weakly. 'You're too late, Doctor. I'm already dead.'

'What?' The Doctor stared at her in horror. As he did, her hands slid out of the sponge and she fell backwards. He caught her in his arms, her head rolling back to face him. 'No …'

'I'm sorry, father,' said Annabelle softly. The chamber blazed with light for a moment, and she smiled at the Doctor gazing down at her. 'I couldn't save them. I couldn't save a single one.' Her smile faded and her shoulders slumped.

The Doctor laid her gently on the shuddering ground. Then he switched on his sonic, revealing the leech still coiled up around her midriff. He grabbed it, and it hissed in anger, opening its mouth wide.

Bill stepped aside to allow the Doctor to make his way outside. She followed him and watched as he stood at the threshold of the sphere and threw the leech into one of the bubbling pools of lava. In an instant, the leech burst into flames and sank beneath the red-hot mud.

Then they returned to the sponge chamber, to find Nardole lying on the quaking floor, whimpering. The Doctor crouched beside him. 'Tell me!'

Nardole looked up. 'It's too much. The pain … is too great. I'm sorry, I can't hold it back any more.'

'You have to try,' said the Doctor. He rubbed his teeth in irritation. 'How long do we have?'

Nardole frowned. 'An hour?'

'A lot can happen in an hour,' said the Doctor. 'Give me back Nardole.'

Nardole blinked as though waking up. 'Ooh. Hello. What have I missed?' The Doctor helped him to his feet as the ground shuddered, forcing Bill to cling to the wall.

'Not much,' said the Doctor. 'Except we're standing on top of a volcano that's about to explode and I have absolutely no idea how to stop it!'

Chapter

14

Sir John Smith was awoken by a hammering on his bedroom door. 'Sir! Sir!'

Smith sat up in bed, rubbing his eyes. The room was in complete darkness, save for the misty moonlight through the window. 'Yes, what is it?'

There was no reply.

'Enter!'

The door creaked open. One of his soldiers appeared, his heavily jowled face lit by the glow of his lamp. 'Sir, sorry to wake ye ...'

'Well, you have done, that is that, now what is it?' said Smith impatiently.

'The ghosts are back.'

'What?' said Smith wearily. This wasn't the first time he'd heard talk of the ghosts. Some of the curfew guard claimed to have seen them walking the streets after dark. Figures in the mist, they said, not responding to their calls. He had put it down to superstition. After all, most of the men serving in the guard were not trained soldiers, but were simple fishermen and shepherds conscripted after the town guard had succumbed to the plague. They had been working night and day for several weeks with barely a few hours' sleep a night. They were having to face death every day, carting the dead to the Muir, while living in constant fear of infection. And, no doubt, they were seeking solace in the bottom of a tankard or two. They could be forgiven for that. He was a forgiving man. But what could not be forgiven was waking him up in the middle of the night. After all, he was still ostensibly recovering from the plague!

'True as I'm stood here,' said the soldier diffidently. 'They're no' walking, though. No' like they were before.'

'Then, pray what are they doing?'

'You should get dressed and see fer yersel, sir,' said the guard. 'Or you winnae believe me.'

'True,' said Smith, climbing out of bed into the chilly night air. He indicated for the guard to bring over his doublet and breeches from the wardrobe. 'Very well. It is time I saw these "discontented spirits" with my own eyes. Then we shall get to the truth of it!'

'Isobel, Isobel. Wake up!'

Isobel could hear her husband calling and, as she slowly drifted back to consciousness, she remembered. Catherine was gone. Her daughter, her baby girl. She would never see her again. Never see her smile, never hear her laugh. No more arguments, no more gossip. And she felt it, an aching hole inside her. A horrible, unfillable emptiness. And she realised there was no longer any reason to go on, no reason to trudge through the days, no reason for living. But go on she must.

'Isobel!' She opened her eyes to find her husband at the foot of the bed, pulling on his shirt by candlelight. It was still dark outside. She was about to ask him why he had disturbed her when the bed shook. And not just the bed. The wooden walls creaked, like a ship in a tempest, and she could hear plates and pots clattering to the floor in the next room. Dust and soot puffed down from the ceiling.

The juddering subsided, and Isobel climbed out of bed and flung on her clothes. 'Tam? What's gaun on?'

Thomas shook his head. 'I dinnae ken. A storm, I think. A great storm.'

She followed her husband into the main room. She could hear the wind wailing and howling across the rooftops, angrily banging the door against its latch. The floor rocked again and the walls creaked ominously, slipping their moorings, and Isobel ran to her husband's arms for support.

'This whole place is gonnae fall,' said Thomas. 'We hae to go.'

'We cannae leave,' said Isobel. 'This is our home.'

'We cannae stay.' Thomas grabbed his coat and placed it around Isobel's shoulders. He opened the door, shouldering it against the freezing wind. Hailstones rattled against the stairwell walls and bounced in through the window. Then two of their neighbours appeared, hurrying downstairs by lamplight. 'Awbody oot!' cried old Hamish Brown. 'The wind's got in the back-attic, it's coming down!'

Isobel took her husband's hand and followed him onto the landing, shielding her face with her other hand while he lit the way with the lamp. The night air was cold and sharp and filled with a righteous fury. Looking outside, Isobel could see the upper stories of the other houses rocking in the wind.

'It's the end o' the world,' gasped Isobel as her husband led her downstairs. 'The Day o' Judgement has come!'

Betsy pulled her shawl around her shoulders and huddled closer to the fire which surged and snapped as the storm gusted down the chimney. Hailstones rattled down the flue pipe like dice and melted in the flames. Outside, the tempest raged, snapping window shutters open and shut, overturning barrels and sending carts to and fro.

Agnes stood at the window, gazing out, her thin grey hair blowing in the breeze. She held her dress about her as though she felt the cold, but Betsy knew she didn't. She was a ghost. She didn't feel the chill in her bones, she had no bones to chill. She just thought she did.

'I've no' seen a storm like it,' said Agnes. 'It's enough to blow half the town away.'

'Come here. Sit down aside me.' Betsy patted the rocking chair by her side.

Agnes reluctantly left the window, sat down and held out her hands to the hearth. 'Betsy,' she said apprehensively. 'I'm feart. This isnae natural.' Her eyes were glistening. 'Take my haunds.'

Betsy shook her head. 'No, I cannae.'

'Please.'

Betsy held out her hands, and Agnes placed her hands over them and smiled thankfully. But Betsy didn't feel a thing. There was nothing there, not even a disturbance in the air.

'At least we're together,' said Agnes. 'After a' we've been through. You and me.'

'Aye,' said Betsy. So why did you leave me, she added to herself. Why did you have to be the first one to go? She looked deep into Agnes's face. She knew every line, every twist of her hair. But she knew, in her heart, that the ghost was not her. It was, she thought, a spirit that had taken her form to comfort her. It was no different from her playing out conversations with Agnes in her mind.

'Betsy,' said Agnes.

'What is it, pet?'

'I cannae feel yer haunds,' said Agnes.

Betsy looked down – to see that Agnes's hands were transparent. She could see her own hands through them. Even as she watched, Agnes's hands faded away.

'What's happenin' tae me?'

Betsy tried to reassure her. 'It's all right. There's no need to be feart.'

Agnes stared at her arms as they turned to mist, her clothing melting away like fog. Her legs had gone too. 'I'm no' real, am I?' she gulped. 'I'm a *ghost*. I'm a ghost!' Her eyes widened and she shook her head. 'I died, didn't I? Oh Betsy, I'm sae sorry, for leaving ye alone …'

'But you didnae,' said Betsy. 'You didnae leave me, did ye?'

Agnes rose from the chair, although by now there was nothing left of her but her head and chest. She turned, as though running to the window … Then there was nothing left of her but swirling smoke.

'Goodbye, ma lassie,' said Betsy softly, looking around her very cold, very empty room. 'I'll miss ye.'

When Smith reached the Netherbow Port, he found a crowd of about a hundred men and women gathered around the gates, shouting and begging to be let out. The gates were locked and half his remaining men stood guard, armed with staffs. There were only thirty of them, all fatigued and grim-faced, worn down by weeks of relentless death and despair.

The guard captain shouted at the crowd: 'Get back! Naebody's leaving!' But the crowd just shoved in further, forcing the guards to lower their staffs to keep them at bay.

Smith caught the guard captain's eye and waved him aside. 'What is this?'

'The ghosts, sir,' said the guard. 'The ghosts, they're aw'where. Look!'

Smith shielded his face against the rain and peered up the High Street, his lips chafing with the cold. At first, he couldn't see what the man was talking about. The sky was overcast and in almost complete darkness, the only light coming from the lamps held by the guards and the gathered crowd. But then he saw the figure advancing down the street. A man in a white nightgown, his cheeks sunken, his eyes like sockets. He shambled towards them, as though about to topple forward … Then he jerked off the ground, like a puppet on strings, his scrawny legs paddling ineffectually beneath him, and he flew up into the air, blown back and forth like a leaf on the breeze. And as he flew overhead, Smith could hear him moaning. A low, abject cry.

In response, the crowd renewed their shouts to be set free. 'It's Judgement Day!' a woman shrieked. 'The deid are leaving their graves!'

And suddenly, out of the fog, more of the figures appeared, whirling in the air, arms flailing, legs cycling, nightgowns and cloaks fluttering behind them. Spun this way and that by the wind, swooping over the rooftops then down into the side streets. Old men and women with wispy white hair on skull-like heads. Husbands and wives cut down in their prime. All those who had been lost to the plague. All with bloodless faces, wild-eyed and wide-mouthed, screaming like the forsaken souls they were.

'Aye,' Smith admitted to the guard who had roused him, raising his voice to be heard over the wind, the screams and the supernatural wails. 'I believe you. There are phantoms.'

'None of the lads hae ever seen them like this afore,' said the guard. 'They normally hirple on, to where it is they're going.'

A skeletal old woman swooped down out of the fog above Smith, causing him to duck. He looked up, but she had gone. She must have disappeared into the darkness.

'Sir,' said the guard. 'What do we do about –' He indicated the terrified crowd at the gate. 'It's the same story at aw' the other ports. Them who can walk are trying to flee.'

Smith's head swirled with a thousand thoughts. This was his town. A town that the Lord had placed under his protection. A town for which so many had given their lives. All that could not be for nothing. But these spirits, this was the Devil's work. Already he could feel a great darkness, an immense weight pressing down on him. Already he could feel the dread in his guts.

Smith came to a decision. 'Open the gates. Let them go.'

'But sir, the quarantine ...'

'You will do as you are told!' shouted Smith. He stared into the driving rain, defying the elements, defying the ghosts, defying creation. 'Tell the men to go around the streets and houses. Put the word out. I'm ordering an evacuation!'

The Psycholops sphere shuddered again, and Bill grabbed one of the overhead branches to stop herself from falling. A harsh, shrieking wind blasted up out of nowhere, flattening her, the Doctor and Nardole against the walls. 'Doctor?' said Bill, but the noise was so deafening she couldn't hear her own voice.

The wind eased as suddenly as it had started. The Doctor unpicked himself from the wall and prowled around the giant sponge.

'It's overloaded, overwhelmed with grief. It's in pain. It's weakening, dying, using up its remaining strength to hold back the eruption. But all this is new. It's frightening, it's panicking. Result: psychic mayhem.'

'It's certainly not happy,' said Nardole.

'That's an understatement,' said the Doctor. 'It's a vortex of misery, a well of grief, a Slough of Despond!'

'And I suppose cheering it up is out of the question?' said Bill.

The Doctor stared at her in disbelief. 'How do you propose we do that? Sing it a happy song? Raindrops on roses? Would you like me to go get my guitar?'

'I don't know. It was only a suggestion.'

'You're forgetting, the Psycholops was already been poisoned by the pre-existing level of grief. This just tipped it over the edge. If the psychic storm isn't just limited to this cave, but extends to the city, what do you think the consequences will be?'

'You tell me.'

'Fear. Hysteria. An all-pervading sense of doom.'

'Which just creates more negative emotions?' Bill realised. 'Like a feedback loop!'

'Exactly. So it may take more than a few verses of "Because I'm Happy" to sort this one out.' The Doctor paused. 'If that's not the correct title for the song, I don't care, it's not relevant right now.'

'Then maybe we should get back to the city? Warn everyone? Start an evacuation?'

'I like that idea,' said Nardole diplomatically.

'That's exactly what the grief-leeches want!' said the Doctor, his voice gaining a patronising tone. 'Didn't you hear Annabelle? They escape the quarantine, spread across the country, take over the rest of your planet.'

'Well, it's better than letting everyone die!' snapped Bill.
'Oh, but we can't, can we? Cos that breaks your precious
Time Lord code! "We can't save a single person"!'

'We can't ...'

'Because we risk "changing established history"!'

'Yes. Because according to established history,
Edinburgh was destroyed in a volcanic eruption in 1645,'
replied the Doctor sarcastically. 'It's in all the history
books. Big, pop-up explodey mountain!'

'Not all books are pop-up, Doctor.' Bill found she
couldn't bear to look at him. She hated him so much right
now. 'Look, I'm going back, even if you're not.' Without
waiting for a reply, she squeezed through the gap in the
chamber wall, pushing aside the branches to emerge into
the cavern.

And stopped. The heat was so intense she thought her
hair would catch fire. The air was so thick with sulphur
it was barely possible to breathe or to keep her eyes
open. The bubbling pools of lava had now formed a lake
covering most of the floor and every few seconds a plume
of lava shot three or four metres into the air, accompanied
by jets of superheated gas.

The ridge leading to the tunnel hadn't been entirely
submerged but it wasn't far off it. It was only about ten
centimetres wide. Bill had a choice. She could edge along it
carefully, or – oh, she couldn't stand the heat. She grabbed
her handkerchief, held it over her nose, and ran along the

ridge, remembering the gymnastics trick of keeping her gaze fixed on a point dead ahead. As she ran, she felt the soles of her shoes heating up, until it was unbearable, but she kept on running …

… until she was across the ridge and back on solid ground. The air was clearer here, as a fresh, cold wind was blowing down the tunnel, enabling her to pause and catch her breath. As she did, she heard a voice calling out.

'Wait!'

She looked back. The Doctor was leaping along the ridge like a sprightly rope-walker, while Nardole followed behind, wobbling precariously with his arms outstretched on either side. Then he paused, losing his nerve. 'No, I'm not doing this,' he shouted across the chamber before scampering back to the sphere. 'Tell you what. I'll wait inside. You can come and get me in the TARDIS.' With that, he ducked into the sphere.

The Doctor stopped, halfway across the ridge. 'Nardole! Nardole!' Then the ridge began to sink into the rising lava. There was no way back.

'Doctor!' yelled Bill. For a moment the Doctor froze, trying to choose whether to go back for Nardole or run to Bill. Then he leapt towards Bill as the ridge was submerged in the fire.

'OK,' said the Doctor once he was with Bill in the tunnel. 'Complication. We now have to go back and rescue Nardole.'

'I'm sure he'll be OK,' said Bill. She pulled out her torch and switched it on.

'His choice,' said the Doctor, breaking into a run.

Bill kept up with him, shivering as another blast of cold air rushed down the tunnel.

'Somebody's left the backdoor open,' muttered the Doctor. Then he halted and gestured for Bill to press herself against the wall. She did, and he flattened himself flat against the wall opposite. Then Bill heard it. The squelching, slithering sound of the leeches. It was getting nearer.

'Torch,' whispered the Doctor.

Bill switched her torch off. He switched off his. Now the only light was the orange glow coming from the volcano chamber.

Then, like a stream of rats, the leeches scurried past. They crawled over each other, jostling for position, hissing and spitting at each other. It was like an oily, wriggling river was flowing down the tunnel and into the volcano chamber, where the leeches disappeared into the molten lava, their bodies catching fire, burning for a moment before sinking beneath the liquid. In less than a minute, they were all gone.

Bill switched her torch back on. The tunnel was empty. 'What was all that about? They were like lemmings!'

'Lemmings don't do that, popular myth perpetuated by unscrupulous wildlife documentary-makers.' The Doctor turned on his torch and continued up the tunnel, walking so quickly that Bill had to half jog to keep up with him.

'But why?' said Bill. 'Why did they do that?'

'I don't know, I suppose they thought people expected to see lemmings jumping off cliffs.'

'I meant the leeches.'

'Oh,' said the Doctor. 'The well of grief. They must've scented it.'

'Got you. So they were drawn to it in a feeding frenzy. Like what drew them to Mary King's Close in the first place!'

'You see? I don't need to explain everything, if you wait long enough, your own little brain will provide you with the answers.'

Bill refused to rise to the insult. 'But that's good, isn't it? If we're rid of the grief-leeches?'

'Only the ones in close proximity will have been affected,' said the Doctor. 'The ones in the city that have taken human hosts, they're the ones we have to worry about.'

'Oh. Still. It'll make getting back a bit easier.'

The Doctor suddenly came to a halt. Bill illuminated his face. He was staring into the distance. 'Which gives me an idea,' he said.

'A plan?'

'Half a plan,' said the Doctor. 'Two-thirds of a plan. Three-quarters. Eight-ninths! Yes!' He sprinted up the passage with renewed urgency. 'It's been bugging me. Niggling away in the back of my mind. It just didn't fit. And you know what I call things that don't fit?'

'Clues!'

'Right,' laughed the Doctor triumphantly. 'Clues. Which lead to solutions!'

'Any chance of letting me know what this plan is?'

'Don't you know?' The Doctor sounded genuinely puzzled. 'After all, it was your idea!'

CHAPTER

15

Chapter
15

The arch of the Netherbow port offered little respite from the wind and hail. The wind was so strong Smith had to hold on to the wall to stop himself behind blown off his feet, while the hail had worked its way through his clothes, freezing his lower back, legs and toes.

The ghosts continued to whirl and swoop overhead, howling, while the crowd continued to grow in number. Most of the people were docile, frightened by the phantoms and worn down by the storm, but a few of the men were becoming belligerent, demanding to be let through. Smith's soldiers held them back at staff-point. Once the outer gate was opened his men would enforce a swift and orderly evacuation. But Smith still hesitated to give the final order. Hoping that the storm would cease, that the ghosts would disappear. That the darkness he felt in his soul would turn to light.

No. That moment would never arrive. If he delayed any longer, there would be a riot and people would be injured. He had no choice. He emerged from the archway, shielding his face from the rain, and approached the guard captain.

He was about to give him the evacuation order when he heard a girl calling out his name.

'Hey! Sir John! Sir John! Hold up!' It was the pretty black-skinned girl, Doctor Stevenson's maid, shoving her way through the crowd to much consternation.

The soldiers looked at Smith expectantly. 'Let her through,' he said. 'Let her through! Let's hear what she has to say.'

The soldiers stepped aside and the girl stumbled over to him, her chest heaving. 'God, so unfit!' She grinned as it took her several seconds to get her breath back. 'Sir John. You can't let them out.'

'What?'

'You have to lock all the gates.'

'But the ghosts. I've already give the order—'

'Un-give it. You have to go back to plan A. Nobody goes in or out. Doctor's orders.'

'The Doctor?'

The girl smiled cheekily. 'You owe him a favour. The magic tablet, remember?'

Smith looked around guiltily. He had made sure it was general knowledge that he had been saved from the plague as proof that his work was part of the Lord's eternal plan. If word got out that witchcraft was responsible …

He beckoned the girl to join him under the archway. Once they were there, he whispered. 'Listen. The town is possessed by spirits. The people are scared out of their wits. If I don't let them leave, there will be hell to pay!'

'Appreciate that,' said the girl. 'But if you let them out, it'll be even worse.' She pulled a device out from beneath her jacket, Doctor Stevenson's 'fumigating torch'. She pointed it at him and it whistled. 'Hold on, I've gotta make sure this only works for you, otherwise things will *really* kick off.'

'"Kick off"?' said Smith.

'Come with me,' said the girl, indicating for Smith to follow her out of the archway to where his soldiers were holding back the shouting, jeering, begging crowd. Then she manipulated the device and pointed it at one of the men in the crowd. He had a leech coiled to his stomach, shimmering in a green light, just like the hideous creature Smith had seen nestling on his own stomach two days ago. Then the girl swung the torch across, and the leech disappeared – and another came into view, clinging to the belly of a young woman. The girl continued to let the green light of the torch move around the crowd, picking out more of the glistening monstrosities. They were attached to nearly every person; the old, the young, children and babes, even some of his own guards.

'Don't worry, they can't see them,' said the girl, switching off the device. 'It's for your eyes only.'

'What *are* those things?' said Smith, horrified.

'Grief-leeches. A kind of infection. Like the plague, but worse, in a way.'

'A plague of leeches?' said Smith. He'd heard of plagues of frogs and locusts. Why should there not be plagues of leeches too?

'Right,' said the girl. 'But right now it's only confined to Edinburgh. It's up to you to stop it getting out. You have to keep the whole town in quarantine. Or they'll spread.'

'I understand,' said Smith. 'And I agree. It is the ... prudent course of action. I shall make sure nobody enters or leaves.'

The girl sighed. 'You know, you're not as bad as I had you pegged, Sir J.'

'Thank you,' said Smith, unsure whether to be flattered or insulted. His mind was still racing with the thought of these creatures, these ... parasites of the soul. 'But if this is a plague, is there any hope for these people?' He recalled seeing the leech on his own stomach. But it had gone away, hadn't it? It was no longer there?

'The Doctor's working on it,' said the girl with a reassuring smile. 'He has a plan. Which is the second thing. We're gonna need to ask another favour.'

Thomas hadn't seen the town so busy for months. As he and Isobel neared St Giles' Cathedral, more and more people abandoned their homes, clutching lamps and dressed in whatever they could pull on over their nightclothes. Old folks hobbled out of their front doors who had not breathed fresh air for weeks. Little children clutched their mothers' skirts. Husbands and wives held each other close. Some people had gathered their valuables and were heading for the gates with handcarts. But most simply huddled into their coats, casting fearful eyes at the night sky.

Thomas felt Isobel's hand tighten as the ground trembled. They kept to the centre of the street as chunks of masonry toppled from the top of St Giles' and slates slid from the tenement roofs. Others took shelter inside the buildings or beneath the carts. Thomas was about to help Isobel beneath one cart when the earthquake faded. His heart pounding, he looked into her tearful, weary eyes, and nodded that they should continue on their way.

One of the town guards ran down the street towards them. 'New orders from the Provost,' he shouted. 'There is to be no evacuation.'

The people mumbled in protest.

'What?' said Thomas. 'But we cannae stay. The ground's shoogling!'

'Aye,' snarled old Hamish Brown. 'An' you only gave out the order a wee while ago!'

'Change of plan.' The guard turned to address the restless crowd. 'Look, it's no' my idea, so dinnae complain to me! All able-bodied men and women are to head to the Luckenbooths. The rest are to keep inside.'

'What?' said Thomas. 'What are we wanted for?'

'Yer tae bring as much stane, bricks or wood as ye can carry.' The guard indicated the pile of rubble that had fallen from the cathedral parapet. 'That'll do for a start.' He waved over a family pushing a handcart. 'And we'll be needing that!'

The husband of the family protested, so the soldier unsheathed his sword. Just the sound of the metal shrieking out of its scabbard was enough to silence the protest. The soldier strode up to the handcart and, to make a point, started dumping the bound piles of clothes and books into the gutter. Then he turned to the crowd. 'Well, don't just stand there. Help! Gather stones, bricks, wood!'

The able-bodied men and women began to do as instructed, while the elderly took care of the babes and children, ushering them indoors. Thomas released Isobel's hand and joined the men picking away at the slabs of rock. He crouched to lift one and heaved it into the cart. Then he heard the screams.

Thomas ran back to Isobel. She was staring up the street, towards the tops of the buildings on the corner of the High Street where a large bird was flapping at the gables. Except, as it swooped down, Thomas realised it wasn't a bird. It was a young woman in a nightdress with long, thick, dark, curly hair. She flew down nearer and emitted an unearthly shriek, like an animal at the slaughter. Then, as she floated into the lamplight, Thomas could see her face, her pale skin, her blank, red-lined eyes.

It was Catherine, their daughter. Or rather her ghost, come to torment them in the street. She floated up into the misty air, and as he watched, she became at one with the fog until there was nothing left.

There were more shrieks and yells of alarm. Further up the street, a dozen or so ghosts were drifting towards them from on high, their cloaks and nightclothes flapping in the gale, their mouths hanging open as they howled.

Something grabbed Thomas's left arm just below the shoulder. 'Thomas,' said a familiar voice.

Thomas turned to see an eagle-eyed face in the lamp glow. 'Doctor?'

'I need you to come with me,' the Doctor said urgently. 'You and Isobel.'

Isobel joined them, a frown on her face. 'But the Provost's orders …'

'They'll cope without you.' The Doctor grinned reassuringly. 'Trust me. This was all my idea. Well, Bill's idea too.'

'What idea?'

'The best way to explain it is to do it. Follow me. Come on! Come on!'

Thomas exchanged a look with Isobel and followed the Doctor. The Doctor darted down a side street in complete darkness, apparently able to see where he was going without a light. Thomas did not share this ability, and held his lamp over his head to illuminate the way. In his other hand he guided Isobel behind him. The Doctor led them through a series of winding, narrow back streets, some so narrow the walls were barely more than a shoulder-width apart. As they ran, rats scurried out of their way, hiding amongst the heaps of rubbish.

Then the ground shook again. Thomas grabbed Isobel and they took cover under an archway. The Doctor dodged under a balcony as slates and chunks of plaster crashed down around them. Then the shaking stopped, and the Doctor waved them on.

'What's happening?' Thomas shouted after him.

'It's quite simple,' the Doctor called back. 'An alien being crashed onto your planet during the last ice age and is now buried under Arthur's Seat. It's highly empathetic and finds grief toxic and all the distress caused by the plague woke it up. Unfortunately, the grief has now got too much for it to bear and it's having a psychic breakdown. Hence all the earthquakes and ghosts. What little willpower it has left is being diverted to prevent Arthur's Seat from erupting like the big, mad volcano it is. Additionally, the alien brought with it a load of malevolent grief-leeches that would quite like Arthur's Seat to erupt because they want everybody to flee which will enable them to spread across

214

the globe feeding on humanity's suffering for evermore. Any questions?'

'Only one,' said Thomas. 'Where you come from, does the word "simple" have a different meaning?'

'Simple is relative,' said the Doctor, coming to a halt.

Thomas and Isobel caught up with him outside a dark blue wooden hut, about eight foot tall. There was writing on the side, but Thomas couldn't read. The Doctor retrieved a key from one of his pockets and placed it in the door of the hut. He grinned. 'Brace yourselves. This is when things may start to get confusing.'

Chapter

16

The ghosts continued to swoop and wail over the High Street but everybody was too busy to pay them close attention. Bill stood with Smith at the entrance to Mary King's Close, making sure the Doctor's plan was carried out. Leaving a guard at the Port, the Provost had sent his men to fetch labour, and now over fifty men and women were in the process of piling up bricks, stones, wooden beams and lumps of upper stories in the street on either side of the alleyway. The volunteers had formed a line, passing stuff forward to be added to the heap, while other men shoved at the mound with shovels and sticks. Already the piles were about two metres high, resembling two bonfires swept up against the walls.

Meanwhile, Smith had despatched two of his city guards into Mary King's Close to remove anyone still lingering there. Since the soldiers had disappeared into the darkness, a dozen or so of the street's wretched occupants had emerged from the gloom, dressed in rags, clutching their few possessions. They were all stick thin, many of them hunched and bow-legged, all of them clearly suffering from the ravages of the plague. Those that could still walk helped those that couldn't, supporting them with arms around their shoulders or carrying them on makeshift stretchers. They were all clearly terrified and desperate, looking around uncomprehendingly as they stepped out into the High Street. At Smith's instructions, nobody informed them of what was planned. Merely that Mary King's Close had to be evacuated of all souls.

Bill checked her phone. It was now thirty-three minutes since the Psycholops had told them they had an hour left. They were cutting it a bit fine. But wasn't that always the way? Bill quickly hid her phone in her pocket, wary of attracting attention. She was getting enough suspicious looks from the locals because of her colour without giving them an excuse to accuse her of witchcraft.

She looked up and down the street. More of the residents were coming to join the effort, shoving carts piled high with debris. And, up in the mist-soaked sky, the ghosts continued to whirl and dart between the rooftops. Every few minutes there was another tremor, and the last one had been followed by what sounded like half a street falling down. It was quite telling that Bill's first reaction had been to order a bunch of men who were standing around doing nothing to go and fetch whatever they could from the ruins. It was only later that she wondered if there had been people in the building when it fell.

Finally, the two guards emerged from the blackness of the alleyway and climbed up the steps to the street level. 'Well?' Smith asked them. 'Is it cleared?'

The bulldog-faced guard nodded. 'Aye. We've checked aw' hames, there's no' a living soul down there.'

'Every house?' said Bill. 'We have to be sure.'

'We got as far down as the close itsel'.'

The other guard, a sallow-faced man of about 19, swallowed. 'There's a feeling down there, Miss. There's ... evil in that place. We wouldnae stay there, no' for aw the King's gold.'

'"The well of grief",' said Bill to herself. The Psycholops' field of misery must have expanded. She could feel it herself. A sensation of a nightmarish blackness rising up out of the earth. A feeling of evil pushing her back. That feeling she'd felt earlier, like having your teeth drilled. It was back, and it was getting stronger.

'If we couldnae linger there, naebody could,' said the bulldog-faced guard.

'According to the neighbours, awbody fled an hour afore,' said the younger guard. 'On my oath, there's naebody down there.'

'OK,' said Bill, biting her lip. 'That's gonna have to be good enough.' She gave the young guard an encouraging smile, and Smith indicated for him to join the others working on the mounds of rubble.

Then, out of nowhere, came a long, low, electronic screech, droning with feedback, followed by an urgent, repetitive chugging. It was a sound Bill would know anywhere, even in mid-seventeenth-century Edinburgh. It was the sound of an electric guitar with the volume cranked up to eleven playing 'How Soon Is Now' by The Smiths.

The crowd gasped and muttered amongst themselves in astonishment. 'Get back to work, the lot of you!' bawled Smith. 'And put yer backs into it!' The men returned to piling up the bricks. Bill dodged through the crowd and ran out into the street, looking past the Old Tolbooth for the source of the bleak, hypnotic sound.

And then, like a rock star at Wembley, the Doctor emerged from the fog, walking slowly and deliberately, strumming at his electric guitar. Wearing his sunglasses even though it was pitch dark. He acknowledged Bill with a nod, then started to sing the verses of the song into his headset microphone, his voice reverberating down the street. He sang mournfully, like he meant every desolate, lovelorn syllable. Moments later, Bill watched as Thomas and Isobel appeared behind the Doctor, both carrying large, black amplifiers, each wired to the guitar. Well, thought Bill with a smile. That explained the volume.

The guitar was so loud it nearly drowned out the other sound. The squelching and hissing sound of thousands of leeches following in the Doctor's wake, like a seething, undulating river of oil. They never got to within two metres of the Doctor – Bill guessed he had set up a force field – but they were clearly desperate to get as close to him as possible, like hungry, slithering Beliebers at a pop concert. As she watched, more leeches slithered rapidly out of the nearby buildings and added to the seething river. Except the river extended into the gloom behind the Doctor as far as Bill could see. No, it wasn't a river. It was a flood. The Doctor was the Pied Piper, but for Hamelin, read Edinburgh; for rats, read grief-leeches; and instead of pipes, the Doctor was busking *The Very Best of The Smiths* on electric guitar.

This was the Doctor's plan. He'd generate his own personal well of grief to draw out the leeches, taking his own emotional baggage and amplifying it to extend across the city. He hadn't actually mentioned the guitar and the Morrissey tribute. Bill wasn't sure they were even necessary. Maybe they helped him get in touch with his feelings. Maybe he needed a way to express those feelings?

But the sunglasses were just the Doctor being the Doctor.

He was walking so slowly that by the time he reached Bill he had come to the end of the song. He struck the strings of the guitar, creating a deafening howl of feedback, then launched into the intro of 'Love Will Tear Us Apart'. As the Doctor moaned his way through the lyrics, Bill heard more leeches screeching. The crowd gathered around the alleyway started in surprise as leeches appeared on their stomachs, only to drop off and slither excitedly over to join the rest of the leeches clustered around the Doctor. The bulldog-faced soldier leapt back in alarm as a leech materialised on his belly, then detached itself in a mass of glue and descended to the ground. Another leech appeared on the young soldier's stomach and slithered away. Everyone in the crowd who had had a leech attached to their stomach – which seemed to be everyone apart from her and the Provost – was suddenly free.

The Doctor led his parade of leeches to the entrance of Mary King's Close. Then he climbed onto the pile of rubble to the right of the alleyway and Thomas and Isobel placed the two amplifiers at his feet. The Doctor created another screech of feedback, and started to pick out a sluggish reggae beat. Recognising the song, Bill grinned to herself. 'Ghost Town'.

All the volunteers stopped their work, staring in horror at the leeches squirming around their feet and staring in bemusement at the Doctor's tribute to Terry Hall and The Specials. Then Bill noticed that as the leeches neared the entrance to the alleyway, they changed direction, scurrying down the steps into Mary King's Close. The Doctor was bringing them within range of the grief generated by the Psycholops! His music and personal grief would lure them to the street, then they would continue down the steep, narrow alleyway, down into the disused baker's, down into the tunnels and eventually down into the lava chamber.

More and more of the leeches slinked down the steps, until they formed a single, black, oily waterfall, a globular mass, all flowing into the darkness as one. The Doctor changed his tune again, this time 'Creep' by Radiohead. This attracted even more of the glistening worms, and they wriggled down the steps too. Then, after a verse and a chorus, the Doctor switched to a song that Bill didn't recognise. It was a heartbreaking melody, somewhere between country and western and a folk song. The Doctor sang it with all his heart. 'My Old Friend The Blues'.

By the time the Doctor reached the second chorus, the river of leeches had thinned to a trickle. Then there were just the stragglers, emerging from the shadows only to scurry into the darkness of the alleyway. Then the final one slithered out of sight, leaving behind only empty cobbles.

The Doctor didn't seem to have noticed. He reached the end of the song, but rather than stopping, he launched into a blues solo, making the instrument whine and shriek with all the feeling he could muster. His fingers tugged at the strings, the pitch rising and rising as the Doctor's playing became more frantic. Soon it became a discordant wail of agony, and then the feedback took over, a Jimi Hendrix screech of distortion, becoming louder and louder until it was deafening.

Fingers in her ears, Bill crept over to Thomas and Isobel and unplugged both the speakers at once. And then there was silence.

Pulled from his reverie, the Doctor suddenly seemed to realise where he was. Bill gave him a meaningful look and the Doctor looked around. Everyone was staring at him open-mouthed with looks of bewilderment and concern.

'Ah, well,' said the Doctor, laying down his guitar. 'I guess you lot aren't ready for that yet.' He lowered his sunglasses and grinned. 'But your great-great-grandkids are gonna love it!'

The Provost stepped forward. 'All right you lot,' he shouted. 'You know what to do. Seal off the close!' And immediately all the volunteers and soldiers set to work, filling the alleyway with the bricks, rocks and wooden beams they had heaped on either side. And, as the alleyway was only a couple of metres wide, the pile mounted up very rapidly.

The Doctor took Bill aside. 'Was the close emptied?'

'Yeah,' said Bill. 'Smith sent a couple of guards to check. There was no one down there. The grief-force thing had already driven them out.'

'"Grief-force"?' said the Doctor with a frown that turned into a smile. 'Your own terminology. Fair enough.'

'What about your half of the plan? How can you be sure you got all the leeches? And what's with the Bono act, anyway?'

The Doctor handed his sunglasses to Bill. 'Try them on.' She did and saw a wireframe image of the street in green on black. Looking down the alleyway, she could see the mass of leeches in luminous bright green. She handed the sunglasses back to the Doctor.

'Grief-leech detectors,' he explained. 'To make sure that none of them escaped my "grief-force".'

'Now That's What I Call Depressing Music,' said Bill.

'The blues,' said the Doctor. 'Don't knock it. Food for the soul.'

He turned his attention to the alleyway. The barrier was now just over a metre high and about two metres deep, extending into the passage as far as the top of the steps. The volunteers shoved on more wood and rubble then soldiers with buckets poured a lump porridge-like substance over the pile, slapping it down into every crack.

'That's it,' shouted the Doctor encouragingly. 'Don't skimp on the daub! It has to be completely watertight. Nothing must be able to get in or out!'

'Don't worry,' said Smith. 'I'll see to that.'

'Good, good,' said the Doctor. 'Keep going. It needs to be blocked off entirely.' He gave the Provost a hard stare. 'And never opened again.'

'I understand. Down there, there's evil.'

'And the rest.' The Doctor turned to Bill. 'How are we doing for time?'

Bill glanced at her phone clock. 'Ten minutes to go.'

'We should move.' The Doctor grabbed his guitar. 'Thomas! Isobel! With me!' Thomas and Isobel acknowledged the Doctor, and, carrying the two amplifiers, they joined the Doctor and Bill at the edge of the gathering.

'Bill?' said a familiar voice. Bill turned to see an old woman with a long thin nose.

'Betsy!' said Bill. 'What are you doing here?'

Betsy indicated the pile of rocks she held in her arms. 'Joining in with the effort, lass.' She smiled. 'When I heard they were sealin' off that den of depravity, I thought I'd lend a haund.'

Bill gave her a grin and patted her on the shoulder. 'You go girl.' The Doctor, Thomas and Isobel were already a dozen metres up the street, running to another of the alleyways. 'Gotta dash,' said Bill, and hurried after them.

Chapter

17

To say Nardole was relieved when the TARDIS materialised in the sponge chamber would be something of an understatement. He hadn't for a moment thought that the Doctor might forget about him; what had worried him was that something might have happened to the Doctor, like a tunnel collapsing on top of him, or some of the locals deciding to lock him up, or burn him for being a witch. The Doctor did have a terrible habit of getting into trouble, mainly because he couldn't help being rude to guards.

Nardole had kept himself occupied. He had moved Annabelle's corpse to the far side of the chamber and covered her face with his coat. He didn't need it any more as the temperature in the chamber was too hot for even his highly developed metabolism. So now he was down to his shirt, using his bobble hat to mop his cheeks and brow.

But then, after exactly fifty-six minutes, he heard the familiar grinding that accompanied the TARDIS's arrival and, moments later, a flashing light appeared about two metres in the air and a very solid, very blue police box appeared beneath it with a firm crunch. The door opened and the Doctor peered out. 'Nardole!'

'Ah, there you are!'

'You'll be pleased to learn I've come up with a plan.' The Doctor leaped out of the TARDIS followed by Bill and, to Nardole's surprise, the two humans, Thomas and Isobel. They looked around with a mixture of fear and disbelief.

'That's nice,' said Nardole, giving the two humans a friendly wave. They didn't wave back. They just stared at him as though he was mad.

'I need you to look after these two good people,' said the Doctor, before turning to address Thomas and Isobel. 'This is all going to be very strange but you have to trust me. You have to stick your hands in … there.' He took Thomas's hands and placed them in the sponge until he was wrist deep. 'And you.' He repeated the process with Isobel.

'You're plugging them into that thing?' asked Bill.

The Doctor nodded, then looked up. 'Psycholops! Are you still with me? I need you to open a psychic link to these two. Access their emotions!'

'Doctor,' said Thomas and Isobel in perfect unison. 'These humans are filled with so much pain. They have lost their daughter. I cannot endure any more.'

'You have to trust me too,' said the Doctor.

'I can't stop the eruption, Doctor. I'm sorry. I can't hold it back.' As Thomas and Isobel spoke, the chamber was plunged into darkness. Then the pulsing orange glow returned but dimmer than before. And the pulsing was growing faster.

'You have to try. For me. Create a psychic channel. Now, put them back on.'

Thomas and Isobel blinked as though waking up. 'What – where?'

'Listen to me,' the Doctor told them. 'Whatever happens, *whatever happens*, you have to keep your hands inside this big sponge. It is vitally important. You have to maintain the psychic link. Do you understand me?'

'No' a word,' said Thomas.

'No, nothing,' said Isobel.

'Excellent—' The Doctor was interrupted by the boom of an earthquake. The chamber shuddered, sending Nardole spinning into the wall. The Doctor remained where he was, a windjammer captain on the high seas. Thomas and Isobel remained with their arms plunged inside the sponge.

'Bill, Nardole. Make sure they don't move,' said the Doctor. And before Nardole could ask him any questions, the Doctor disappeared inside the TARDIS. An instant later, the light on the top flashed and it disappeared.

Nardole looked at Bill to ask what to do. By way of an answer, she gripped Isobel's wrists to make sure the woman

229

kept her hands stuck into the sponge. Following her lead, Nardole gripped Thomas's arms, held him in position, and waited for whatever was going to happen next.

The Doctor sat on the stairs of Annabelle's house, staring down into the hallway. It was in complete darkness, and, apart from the occasional creak as the building settled in the night, there was complete silence. Because this was the night before. He had travelled back in time in the TARDIS to sit on these stairs.

A key turned in the lock and the door creaked open. Caught in the moonlight was a figure. A figure with a wide-brimmed hat, a long cloak and a mask in the shape of a raven's skull.

The Doctor watched as the Night Doctor locked the door behind it and placed the key on a nail in the wall. Next, it removed its hat and placed it on a hook. It pulled back its hood, to reveal no head beneath, then carefully lifted off the raven's skull mask and hung it up. It took off its gloves, and finally the cloak floated over to the hooks and hung itself up.

The Doctor counted to fourteen and switched on his torch. Then he hurried down the stairs and, as swift as a cat burglar, he gathered all the parts of the plague doctor's outfit.

Nine days earlier, the Doctor stood in the shadows wearing the plague doctor's outfit. It was extremely claustrophobic and his vision was limited to two small eyepieces, like looking out through the bottom of two stained-glass tumblers. Worst of all was the combined smell of the oil-soaked cloak and the contents of the beak strapped to his face. It was packed with dried heather, honeysuckle and other herbs, and the resulting scent was so cloying the Doctor chose to breathe through his mouth. And, in the tight, black space of the mask, all he could hear was his own half-suffocated breathing, rasping and sighing in his ears.

He stood in the darkness for several minutes, watching the door of the tenement where Thomas and Isobel lived. The place where he and Nardole had first met Catherine's ghost. But, right now, up on the eighth floor, the young girl was still clinging on to life.

The Doctor didn't have to wait long. The door opened, and through the distorting lenses of the mask he saw the Night Doctor emerge from the tenement. The Night Doctor looked left and right as though scenting the air, then glided away, its cloak not touching the ground. As it passed the Doctor, it appeared to stretch and pool as though made of viscous liquid, then it floated away into the night.

The Doctor watched it go. Then he waited. Two hours he had been told, so two hours it would be. He counted to seven thousand two hundred. Then, at last, he walked over to the tenement, opened the door, and made his way up the stairs, hearing them creak and bend under his weight. He reached the eighth floor and approached the Abneys' door. Then he knocked on it with his gloved right hand, hard, four times.

After a pause, the door opened and Thomas appeared in the fisheye-lenses of the mask. He looked exhausted, weather-beaten, his red-lined eyes filled with helpless desperation.

The Doctor indicated with a wave of his hand for Thomas to stand back and he obeyed. The Doctor ducked under the doorway and walked into the centre of the room, looking around until Isobel and her daughter slid into view.

'What is it?' demanded Thomas, his voice muffled by the mask. 'You've already seen her, what dae you want?'

The Doctor ignored him and approached Catherine. She lay in a bed by the fireplace, her eyes closed, her skin as white as death. Her forehead and hair were soaked with perspiration. The Doctor leaned over her for a better view.

'No,' begged Isobel from behind him. 'You cannae. You cannot take her.'

The Doctor did not reply. He wished he could give them some words of comfort but he couldn't. He drew back the blankets, reached down, and gently lifted Catherine from her bed.

Bill gripped Isobel's wrists tightly, making sure the woman's hands remained inside the sponge. Isobel stared at her in confusion and shock. Bill gave Nardole a meaningful look, and Nardole held Thomas's arms in place. Then Bill waited as the chamber darkened and lightened and the floor trembled.

Barely five seconds after it had disappeared, the TARDIS reappeared in the same spot with a wrenching, shrieking sound. Bill felt Isobel tense in fear; she'd never seen the TARDIS materialise before. Then the doors began to open, and it was Bill's turn to feel tense, as she knew what was coming next.

'Ma. Pa.' Catherine stood in the TARDIS doorway, the Doctor beside her. She was smiling, a sardonic twinkle in her eyes. She was a picture of good health, with blushing cheeks and lips as red as freshly cut roses. She had no scars or blisters and her long, dark hair flowed down her back, as clean as her spotlessly laundered nightgown. Bill noticed she was wearing a pair of fluffy slippers.

'Cathy?' said Isobel, turning to face her. As she did, Bill felt her hands withdrawing from the sponge and held them firmly in place. By now, the whole chamber was shuddering. 'Cathy?'

'Naw. She's a ghost,' said Thomas fearfully. 'Another ghost.'

'Not this time,' said the Doctor. 'Thomas, Isobel. This is your daughter.'

Isobel stared at her, struggling to take in what she saw. 'Can it be?'

'It's me, ma,' said Catherine gently. 'Flesh and blood.'

'But you had the plague,' said Thomas.

'I ken.' Catherine smiled at her father. 'I got better.' She glanced back at the Doctor. 'The Doctor … the Night Doctor came for me, and took me for treatment. There were these sisters, what looked like cats—'

'Let's not go into that right now,' said the Doctor. 'Go to them.'

Catherine strode over to her mother even as the floor continued to shudder. As she did, a deep rumbling and crashing came from outside. Bill guessed the cave roof was falling in. Then Catherine reached out a hand, and touched her mother on the cheek.

'It's really you,' said Isobel, shaking her head in disbelief. 'You're alive. Oh my sweet lass, you're alive!'

'I didnae die,' said Catherine. She looked to the Doctor for guidance, and he prompted her to go her father. She reached out and touched Thomas's arm. 'It's me.'

'Oh, Cathy,' said Thomas, the words choking in his mouth. 'We've missed ye. Ye cannae ken how we've missed ye … Our wee lass.'

Nardole was still holding Thomas's hands in the sponge. If he hadn't been, Thomas would have hugged his daughter. Instead, it was down to her to hug him. She put her arms around his chest and buried her face in his shoulder. Thomas looked down at her, cheeks streaming with tears.

Bill looked back at Isobel. She was looking at her daughter with tearful eyes, filled with such love, such devotion, such relief, like Bill had never seen. The purest, greatest joy. The love of a mother for her daughter.

Then the chamber filled with bright orange light and the floor stopped shaking. But, Bill noticed, the rumbling outside was still going on.

'You can let them go now,' said the Doctor.

Bill released Isobel, and stood back as Isobel crossed to embrace her daughter and her husband. Nardole let go of Thomas's wrists, giving him a supportive smile.

And for a moment, Bill just watched them. Isobel's body was shaking with sobs and Thomas was holding his daughter so tight, he might never let her go again.

Bill turned to see the Doctor running his hands over the nodes and branches of the central sponge. 'It worked?'

The Doctor nodded. 'An influx of unadulterated happiness.'

'Which was my idea,' Bill pointed out.

The Doctor winked as an acknowledgement. 'It seems to have just about stabilised the psychic field. Nardole, would you mind …?'

'Not at all,' said Nardole, gazing up at nothing in particular. Then he spoke in a daydreamy voice. 'Doctor. The pain … the pain has been eased. Where there was grief, now there is … hope.'

'Never mind getting in touch with your feelings!' said the Doctor. 'Just tell us! Have you got your strength back?'

'Can you stop the volcano going off?' said Bill, getting to the point.

Nardole looked at her sadly and shook his head. 'No. I can't.'

'What?'

'The pressure is too great.'

'What?'

'But if I vent some of the pressure … I might be able to prevent a *full* eruption.'

Nardole looked at the Doctor, as though to ask for permission.

The Doctor gritted his teeth and sighed. 'Well, it looks like we don't have any choice, so go for it, big man! Vent away!'

The men of the town had sealed off Mary King's Close to a height of ten feet, creating a solid wall of rock and stone six feet thick. They were in the process of reinforcing it with buttresses when the ground shook. The barrier remained firm, but as the ground continued to shake further, panic gripped the crowd and cries of alarm filled the air.

'Back, all of you!' shouted Smith to the men still working on the barrier. 'It's coming. Get back!' The men and soldiers stepped back from the wall of rock. Smith looked up nervously. The buildings on either side of the alleyway were ten storeys high. If they collapsed, nobody in the street would be safe. Luckily it was still raining, so there was no chance of fire.

It was only then that Smith noticed something was missing. The ghosts had disappeared. In all the commotion of building the wall, he had stopped paying them any attention. And now there was no sign of them, up or down the street, and not a single cry or wail could be heard.

The ground shuddered again, like a great beast stirring from its sleep. Then there was a deafening crashing sound, a massive, heart-pounding boom of thunder ... and from the depths of Mary King's Close a vast fireball burst into the sky, sending black smoke high into the clouds. The fire continued to spout out of the darkness, an orange-burning flame, rising over the rooftops before slumping back into the shadows. Moments later, the rain was joined by small chunks of black stone rattling on the cobbles, some of them smouldering, some still glowing red hot and hissing with steam as they landed in the puddles. The volunteers ran for shelter beneath the archways of the Luckenbooths, and Smith shielded his face with his hat and ordered his men to move further back.

The plume of smoke continued to stream into the heavens but the fire fell back. But then there was a second rumble. The storm had passed, and now the thunder was coming from a mile away to the East. Smith turned to look down the High Street where he could see the first orange glow of dawn in the distance. Except it was too early for dawn. The orange glow was not the sun. It was coming from the summit of Arthur's Seat. And, as he watched, what looked like molten gold spurted out of the mountain, and a web of golden rivers appeared trickling down its side.

The crowd cowered and gasped. Smith could feel his heart pounding. But, almost as suddenly as it had begun, the ground stopped shaking, and after a few minutes nothing but smoke was rising from the mountain. It was over.

Chapter

18

Isobel and Thomas had insisted on them staying for breakfast, so Bill found herself sitting by their hearth, warming her hands on a bowl of porridge. It didn't taste too bad and certainly helped make her feel less bleary-eyed after a night without sleep. The Doctor tucked into his porridge with relish, but when Isobel offered some to Nardole, standing by the window, he apologetically patted his tummy while mouthing 'calories'. So Isobel returned to the fire, and as she did she walked past her daughter seated there and stroked her hair. Catherine looked up and gave her mother a rose-cheeked smile.

'Isn't it cheating, though?' asked Bill. 'To pop back like that?'

The Doctor scraped the bowl for the remains of the porridge. 'Not at all. I was merely ensuring events followed their established course. We knew the Night Doctor called a second time and took Catherine away. Which always struck me as odd.'

'A clue.'

'Quite. It didn't fit in with its *modus operandi*.'

'You've brought our Cathy back tae us,' said Isobel. 'For which we will forever be grateful.'

'Not just that,' said the Doctor, handing Isobel the empty bowl and getting to his feet. 'You see, Catherine wasn't just cured. She now has a genetically engineered bacteriophage coursing through her system.'

'Don't worry,' said Bill. 'I don't know what he's talking about either.'

'It means Catherine's immunity can be passed on to others,' explained the Doctor. 'Just like an infection.'

'And how's it "passed on"?' said Thomas suspiciously.

'Physical contact,' said the Doctor. 'A brief handshake should do it.'

'You mean, anyone I touch … will be cured?' said Catherine.

'And those who aren't infected never will be. You should be able to rid this whole town of the plague in a couple of days.'

'But I cannae do that,' said Catherine. 'I cannae go round people's houses, asking to be let in. If they have the plague, they'll no' let anyone cross their doorstep.'

'Oh, I think they will. You just need to dress the part.' The Doctor nodded to Nardole, who popped into the back room and returned carrying a cloak, a pair of gloves, a wide-brimmed hat and raven's skull mask. Nardole handed the bundle to Catherine.

'The plague doctor?' said Catherine. 'You wish me to be the town plague doctor?'

'There's a vacancy,' said the Doctor. 'Annabelle Rae started the job, now you can finish it. Do her proud, Catherine. Be a doctor.'

Catherine turned the mask over in her hands, peering into the eye sockets, then looked to her parents for their opinion. 'I can really save the whole town, just like that?'

'You not only can, you have to,' said the Doctor. 'You see, I've kind of made a promise …'

'So what was all that stuff about not changing history?' said Bill cheekily. 'How we couldn't save even just one person?'

'All true,' said the Doctor. 'I'm a Time Lord, I get to call these things.'

'Where to draw the line?'

'Exactly. And I draw it at … one city. One small, human city.'

'But you've changed history,' said Bill. Ahead of them, down the High Street, she could see Arthur's Seat in the cold light of dawn. Smoke continued to pour out of the top of the mountain, joining a thundercloud streaking away into the distance. 'I don't remember there being anything in the history books about a volcano erupting.'

'I made a deal,' said the Doctor, resuming their brisk walk. 'The Psycholops can't hold back a full eruption if the ambient level of grief continues to mount. So, no more deaths from the plague. Full stop.'

'Yeah, and how isn't that changing history?'

'The number of cases went into a steep and unexplained decline around now. Maybe I haven't changed things at all. Maybe this is how it was always meant to be?'

'Yeah, you keep telling yourself that.'

'And besides,' said the Doctor, grinning conspiratorially. 'It's better than the alternative, of Edinburgh being destroyed by a volcano in 1645. Now that really would be noticed. Even as far south as England.'

'But people are gonna remember. It'll be in all the history books.'

'No. That's the another part of the deal. In return for reducing the amount of grief, the Psycholops is generating a low-level amnesia field. People will slowly forget everything that happened. The ghosts, the eruption.'

'Won't they notice?'

'It'll be a gradual process, over years, generations. Imperceptible. And they'll fill the gaps with ghost stories of their own. Within five years, ten, everything will be back to normal.'

As the Doctor spoke, they came to the entrance of Mary King's Close where the Provost was directing a group of soldiers to build a second wall across the alleyway. The Provost raised a hand in acknowledgement of the Doctor, Bill and Nardole. Bill gave him a little wave in reply.

'What about the grief-leeches?'

'All gone. Wiped out when the volcano was vented.' The Doctor shrugged. 'Assuming there isn't another colony elsewhere on the planet. Something to keep an eye out for.'

'And the ghosts?'

'The Psycholops may create one or two from time to time, to keep people of out harm's way. But on the whole, we should have seen the last of them.'

Bill stopped, causing the Doctor and Nardole to halt. 'Look, you two go ahead, I'll meet you at the TARDIS,' she said. 'Just got one last thing to do.'

Bill knocked on the door of Betsy's house. As she waited, she took one final look around the square. Although there was still rubbish heaped against the walls, and it still smelt like the canteen's bins, in the fresh light of day it seemed brighter, warmer. As though the grief that had been pressing down on the city had finally been lifted.

A key turned in the lock and Betsy opened the door. 'Ah, Bill. Come in if you're coming.'

Bill followed her up the stairs into her room. 'Thanks for mucking in last night.'

'The least I could dae,' said Betsy stiffly. 'I hear the close is to be sealed for good. No' afore time.'

'Yeah,' said Bill. 'The Provost is gonna find the people who lived there new places to live.'

'Aye. There's nae shortage of rooms going spare.' Betsy sat down in her chair and indicated for Bill to sit.

Bill remained standing. 'Have you seen Agnes at all, since last night?'

Betsy shook her head. 'No. No, she's away. It was good of her, sending me the ghost. But I ken it wasnae her.'

'You knew?'

'When you've been with someone forty years, you'll understand. See, I can still hear her gabbin' in here.' Betsy tapped the side of her head. 'Any time I want. She'll aye be with me. My sweet Agnes.'

'What's this?' said a voice from the door. 'You gossiping about me again?'

Bill turned to see Agnes standing in the doorway. But she looked different this time. She seemed ... brighter. Like she was subtly glowing.

'Agnes?' said Betsy.

Agnes stepped forward and smiled regretfully. 'I've come to say goodbye. I've been given word that it's time tae go.'

Betsy rubbed something from her eye. 'You? You were never one for the goodbyes.'

Agnes approached her. 'I didnae say it before, did I? Before I passed on. So I'm here to say it now.'

She stepped forward, and put out her arms to embrace Betsy. And Betsy reached out to embrace her, and although Agnes was just a ghost and as insubstantial as thin air, the two women held each other tight.

Bill brushed away a tear and slipped quietly away.

The High Street was jam-packed with tourists of every nationality. Students with unwieldy, brightly coloured backpacks took selfies with each other, while pensioners in plastic poncho raincoats consulted their guidebooks for directions and points of historical interest. In the middle of the street, two performers on stilts hurled skittles back-and-forth. As they added another skittle, and another, the gathered crowd broke into applause.

Bill looked around, taking in the sights, the endless faces, the excited clamour of music and laughter. Three hundred and seventy-two years later, the High Street was almost entirely unrecognisable. The Old Tolbooth and the Luckenbooths had gone. The bulging, squeezed-together ten-storey buildings were now solid buildings of grey stone a mere seven storeys high. St Giles' Cathedral was still there, of course, but apart from that, there was virtually nothing left of the old town.

'I got you here in the end,' remarked the Doctor beside her.

Bill looked down the High Street in the direction of Arthur's Seat but it was no longer visible. A series of banners announcing the festival flapped in the wind. 'And the Psycholops? It's still under Arthur's Seat?'

The Doctor nodded. 'Still there. Still holding back the volcano. And still empathically attuned to the people of Edinburgh.'

'What, you mean, it's still feeling whatever everyone here is feeling?'

'Yes,' said the Doctor. 'But it should be OK. I've put in place one or two things to ensure the local population are never too miserable for too long.'

'Such as?'

'All this.' The Doctor gestured, indicating the crowds, the colourful banners, the jugglers. And Nardole, who had wandered over to join the jugglers while Bill wasn't looking, and who was now happily joining in with the show, juggling four skittles at once. 'Plus a knees-up and a sing-song every new year.'

'You never invented Hogmanay,' laughed Bill. She couldn't tell whether he was joking.

'I probably did,' said the Doctor, gazing enigmatically into the distance. 'It's got my fingerprints all over it. I've always wanted to go back and check.'

'And you did *not* invent the Edinburgh Festival.'

'Well, somebody did. And as long as the general level of happiness keeps being topped up to compensate for the general level of Scottishness, the Psycholops will be happy too.'

'It won't mind, being stuck under a mountain for the rest of time?'

'No,' said the Doctor. 'It told me it rather likes it.'

'Flyer?' said a voice in her ear. Bill turned and a young, bright-faced girl with dark, wavy hair offered her a leaflet.

Bill took it without thinking and the girl moved on through the crowd. Bill watched her go, thinking she reminded her of someone, then glanced down at the leaflet:

Ghost Tours – The Real Mary King's Close

Nah, thought Bill, crumpling up the flyer. I think I'll give that one a miss.

Acknowledgements

Any journey into history means research, and in writing this novel I was particularly indebted to Robert Chambers' account *A Tale of the Plague in Edinburgh* and Robert Louis Stevenson's *Edinburgh: Picturesque Notes*. For the geography of Edinburgh I referred to James Gordon's 1647 map of the city (which can be viewed on the National Library of Scotland website), while for the buildings I referred to *Lost Edinburgh* by Hamish Coghill, along with innumerable websites. My intention was not to write an historically accurate account of the plague – any story where the TARDIS turns up is unlikely to be entirely accurate – but just to try to make sure that everything I got wrong I got wrong *deliberately*, for the sake of the story, rather than out of ignorance.

I am also indebted to my Scottish Dialogue consultants Margaret Brown, Nisbet Bryce, Robert Dick and Andrew Smith. I have strived to make the language as authentic as possible but have inevitably had to make some compromises for the sake of clarity, so please could Scottish readers bear in mind that the TARDIS translation circuits are not *completely* infallible.

And finally, and most importantly, my thanks to Debbie Hill, for all her help, criticism and support.